RED
VELVET
CRUSH

CHRISTINA MEREDITH

RED
VELVET
CRUSH

Greenwillow Books
An Imprint of HarperCollinsPublishers

Red Velvet Crush
Copyright © 2016 by Christina Meredith
All rights reserved. No part of this book may be used or reproduced in any manner whatsoever without written permission except in the case of brief quotations embodied in critical articles and reviews. Printed in the United States of America. For information address HarperCollins Children's Books, a division of HarperCollins Publishers, 195 Broadway, New York, NY 10007.
www.epicreads.com
The text of this book is set in Joanna MT.
Book design by Sylvie Le Floc'h
Library of Congress Cataloging-in-Publication Data is available.
ISBN 978-0-06-206227-7 (trade ed.)
16 17 18 19 20 PC/RRDH 10 9 8 7 6 5 4 3 2 1
First Edition
 Greenwillow Books

For Hamid

The door to our room is cracked open, out of habit mostly, because Billie was so afraid of the dark when we were little. I don't mind anymore.

Light shines in from the kitchen and makes a soft golden triangle on the faded pink rug between our beds, same as it did back when my mom's humming would lull us both to sleep while she paged through a magazine or mindlessly flipped through the channels on the TV, snapping through them all once before beginning again, always searching, as if something new were going to appear, like magic.

Dad waits at the kitchen table, his nightly vigil under way.

His arms are crossed over his chest. His eyes are unfocused, stubborn. Fresh scrapes shine from under his chair, a new layer dug into the marks already there. His coffee grows cold.

Eventually I hear the chair scuff across the floor and the mug clink into the bottom of the sink. He is giving up. Giving in.

I turn and squint into the light as he shuffles across the linoleum. His shoulders are square and strong. He moves carefully, a big man in a small kitchen.

My bed creaks and he pauses, hand above the light switch.

His eyes lock onto mine. He sighs, heavy, and clicks off the light.

I lie alone in the dark, eyes open long after he leaves for bed, long after I should, long past the point of remembering things that help, only things that hurt. I keep still, listening for Billie's breathing coming from across the room, even and thick, so I can drop off to sleep. But she is gone. There is only the sound of wind outside my window.

Tucking my covers in tight under my chin, I slide into a mental space that I only allow myself to find in bed, alone, wrapped in the safety of my sheets. Both my parents are there, happy and together. My brother, Winston, is there, and Billie, too, who seems less annoying late at night when I am sleepy and eager to drift off and dream.

I picture them all with me, lost in time, holding hands as the stars sparkle above us. I start to fade, lifting up and away from everything that holds me here, obeying the laws of gravity and cooking hamburger for dinner on a Saturday night, again.

an endless blue

1

"Winston," Dad says, coming in through the front door with a stomp just as I set dinner on the table.

Winston slides into the chair facing mine and looks up. His hands are washed. His dark blond hair is parted and combed. He has on his favorite long-sleeve T-shirt with the hula girl on the front. Her boobs spill out the sides of her bikini top and make me want to blush.

Winston is making an unexpected appearance at the dinner table. He's usually out on Saturday nights, out in the garage, or out chasing down a car part, or out just being Winston, drifting and driving.

"Could you stop sleeping with the neighbors' daughters?" Dad asks, his voice gravelly. He blanches before he turns back to give the door a heavy shove with his boot.

Winston barks a smoky laugh and angles a taco over his plate. He hunches his shoulders, cracking into the shell.

"I didn't sleep with her," he replies, a sly smile playing across his lips as my dad pulls out the chair at the head of the table. "Let's just say she has very soft hands."

I look across the table at Winston in disbelief. Shreds of lettuce are hanging from the corners of his mouth. Hot sauce oozes over his chin.

My bite of taco scratches all the way down.

Most of the time I try to think of Winston as a very tall eunuch, so the fact that Carmen from next door, who is just a grade above me, has hooked up with him—probably right there on our couch—well, gross.

"Jailbait . . ." Billie sings.

She is busy picking the lettuce out of her taco until it is just sad, burned meat and shell.

Winston snorts. "That would be a great name for a band."

I reach over his plate for the hot sauce.

"Speaking of bands . . ." he says, grabbing the hot sauce and holding it hostage. He raises his eyebrows at me.

"We weren't really," I say, pulling the bottle free and giving it a shake.

Winston has a new job at the local radio station. It's housed in a small, dirt-colored building out on the highway, with a gravel parking lot and an old electric transformer planted out back. Ever since the day he started he's been begging me to stop by.

"Come on, Ted . . ." He nags, his mouth full again, "Come down to the station and meet the boys. Maybe bring your guitar."

I picture a bunch of old dudes in desperate need of haircuts trapped inside, talking low and loud, inviting me down to the racetrack on Sunday, Sunday, Sunday, all while surrounded by half-eaten bags of Cheetos.

"I'll pass," I say.

Winston sets his taco on his plate and stares down at the table.

"Ted," he finally confesses, "I already played your thing for Randy."

"What thing?"

"That thing you made with Billie, in the garage. Your demo thing."

"Who's Randy?" Billie asks.

Billie should know this by now. Randy owns the radio station. He's got a big Ford truck, a weak FM signal, and some family money (at least the chunk that he didn't drink away before he joined AA). He inherited the title of program director along with the station and has apparently taken a shine to Winston. Randy seems to think that Winston has potential—and an unlimited supply of cigarettes. One of these is true, so he hired Winston on the spot. He is like Winston's new guardian angel.

"I do not have a demo thing," I say.

"Well, that's what he called it."

"That was just, you know"—I rock onto the back legs of my chair as my hands fumble in the air for what it was—"goofing around."

Winston dusts his fingertips clean and watches me land. "Well, Randy liked it. And he'd like a second listen."

I'm not sure I wanted him to have a shot at a first one.

"He said that?" Billie asks.

It's not like she did anything that day in the garage. She just hit some buttons. I could do that myself—I have—but nobody, not even Billie, knows about that one.

"He did." Winston nods, as if Randy's opinion were some kind of stamp of approval. Oh, the old guy who smokes a lot and used to be addicted to cough syrup? Yeah, well, he likes your songs, so you're all set.

"Randy likes to invest." He shrugs as he finally wipes the hot sauce from his face, thank God, and gets up from the table. "You've got talent. He's got money. I see opportunity."

I watch as Winston walks across the kitchen with his plate in one hand and the mostly empty milk jug in the other.

The last opportunity Winston saw left us with five cases of instant shake mix that promised we were "Guaranteed to Lose Weight!" The cardboard boxes still line the bottom of our hall closet years later. Winston never sold a single packet, and all we lost was $250.

Dad pushes at his shirtsleeves and, quietly listening, reaches for the last taco.

"You don't have to do anything," Winston promises, his skinny butt sticking out of the fridge while he finds a place to stash the milk. "But what if I get some people together?" His long arm stretches out and drops his plate into the sink. He snags the dish towel hanging from the handle on the stove and turns to face me, "What if we could make some cash?"

"You mean what if *you* could?"

Because this isn't about me. Not really. How much cash can I make? I've never been in a band, never even set foot on a real stage. I'm not even legal. I'd be better off at Hooters. At least I already have all the right equipment for that.

Dad remains silent during Winston's entire pitch, apparently in full support of whatever it might take to keep his only son employed and accounted for, even if it is only part-time, even if it is something as sketchy as pimping his little sister out in a rock 'n' roll band.

I am almost with him, remembering the years when Winston kind of went missing. He skipped a lot of school. Dad bailed him out on a regular basis. Process servers and suspicious characters knocked on our door at all hours.

Dad used to wander around a lot and ask, "Where's your brother?"

Billie and I would shrug.

"Have you tried juvie?" I'd ask, and he'd grump and grumble away, his socks slipping across the cracked linoleum.

Maybe he is hoping that is all behind us now. That Winston is finally walking the straight and narrow and Randy is our beer-bellied salvation.

Truth is, we could use the help.

Dad is already working a second job on the night shift at the local warehouse, stacking pallets and other manual work that he is entirely too old to do, and things are still tight around here, as evidenced by the wilted lettuce on our tacos and the watered-down hot sauce.

Dad rolls his shirtsleeves down, his two tacos finished. I wait. His opinion is the one that matters; he is the only grown-up we have left.

My mom left us back when I was in the second grade. Mrs. Brewer was lumbering through a set of flash cards as a gusty autumn wind pushed the tire swing against its frame outside my classroom window.

Bump, bump, bump . . . 11 times 12 was 132. Bump, bump, bump . . . 12 times 12 was 144. Bump, bump, bump, while my mother packed a bag, swung the front door shut, and walked away on a sunny Tuesday afternoon.

Billie and I came home to a quiet house that day, which in itself wasn't unusual, but it was also empty. No smoke drifted from my mother's room, no mumbled phone conversation dragged on behind her closed door as we ate cookies right from the bag, trying to hear what she was saying, chewing as quietly as humanly possible.

We were always trying to figure out what was going on with her. Everybody was.

"I don't think she's coming back this time," Dad said to Winston as I watched from my bed that night, the door to our room left open wide.

He was leaning against the kitchen counter, a coffee mug in his hand, his eyes on the night sky and the empty clothesline in the backyard.

Winston sat at the table, taking the news like a little man, much better than Billie or me. He was twelve.

I never once saw him cry. But I bet he did.

Lying behind me, tight against my back, scared and shaky, Billie's breath hitched and caught in her chest. A flutter of air escaped from her, and a ragged leftover cry crept up my spine.

Billie took it the hardest.

She was only five then; she didn't remember a time before the fights or the heavy silence and tension that hung over our house like a dark cloud.

I did, but I was caught somewhere in the middle, between Winston and Billie, straddling stony silence and tragic heartbreak.

As far as I know, my mom didn't have delusions of

grandeur or talent that went wasted by the wayside. She just wanted to get out. Out of the small town she was born in. Out of the little life that she had lived until the age of eighteen.

She did have a bad case of wanderlust and a serious caffeine addiction.

They kept her up late at night thinking, smoking. Staring out the windows of our boxy little house, her eyes glassy as the channels clicked by, trying to see past the flat gray sky to something better, to that unknown oasis of fun or adventure or whatever it was just over the horizon. To something that made her feel whole, stable, and maybe settled. That stopped the churning of her thoughts and quieted her nonstop tuneless humming.

Maybe my mom had music in her head, but she didn't know what to do with it. She didn't pick up the guitar, or get obsessed with albums, or join the church choir.

She didn't curl up with a wrinkled notebook, filling page after page, fashioning a never-ending stream of dreams and hurts and secrets into songs. Not like I do.

Instead she sat and chain-smoked menthol cigarettes, hummed constantly, and played the piano once or twice a year. The rest of the time her tune was trapped, churning around in her head, like electricity—with no outlet.

She didn't leave a note or anything.

She simply called Dad at work, broke the news, and then

slipped out the door before he could drive home. She was in a hurry, I guess.

For years we set the table for her, one empty plate and one empty glass left at the foot of the table at the end of every night. We've never even scooted over to fill up that empty space. We just pretend it isn't there.

Billie's next to me now, arranging bits of taco meat in a circle around the edge of her plate. The mom end of the table is empty, like always, and Winston's leaning against the counter with a towel trapped in one wet hand, waiting for me to respond.

Somehow his request to stop by the station has snowballed into the start of a band, complete with mountains of cash and the expansion of Randy's investment portfolio. How did that happen?

I look over at Dad. He rubs his face with his hands and sits back in his chair.

"Does this mean you'll keep your hands off the neighbors?" he asks Winston.

Winston grins and crosses his heart. "Scout's honor."

We all know Winston left the Scouts when he discovered a skunk in the bathroom at day camp. Rumor has it he peed his pants on the way home. I can't be sure, though. Mom was still around to do the laundry in those days.

Dad pushes his plate away and nods at me: permission granted.

But it is up to me to decide.

"So, like a band?" I ask Winston. Might as well start at the very beginning, I think. We can get to the mountains of money later.

Winston shrugs his big shoulders again, easing me into the idea. "I could send out an e-mail from the station, set up some auditions, maybe put up a posting."

Do I want Winston hunched over a creaky keyboard at the station, jabbing away with his oil-stained fingers, arranging my future? Seems like there must be more refined ways to break into the music business. Like sledgehammers or monster trucks.

"Maybe you could play some local clubs once you get practiced up," he says, pulling a twenty-dollar bill out of his front pocket and unfurling it. "Get to know some of the presidents we never covered before Mr. Hansen curled up and died."

Winston doesn't know that Mr. Hansen was replaced years ago. Besides, I doubt that we'll see many bills bigger than a twenty. More like lots of singles. Stripper money. We will probably only make enough money to buy some new guitar picks—if we're lucky.

"Come on, Ted," Winston says as he wipes his hands on the dish towel and tosses it onto the counter. The towel slides to the floor.

"I'll think about it," I say, but not believing that I ever actually will.

Mostly I want this conversation to be over, for Billie and Dad to be doing something other than staring at me with hope and expectation, just waiting for the second when I cave and do what Winston wants. What everyone wants.

"Fair enough," Dad replies, and gets up.

He crosses the room and struggles into his brown Carhartt coat, the one with the flannel lining, that I'd love to borrow and never give back, his mind already on the task ahead of him, a night of lifting and stacking and cold, stiff shoulders.

"What are you doing tonight?" Dad asks Winston, pausing at the door.

"Going out."

"Billie?"

"Going out."

He looks at me.

"Staying in," I say.

We all know that going out means driving up and down the main street until somebody finds a place to have a party, and then everyone converges. It meant the same thing back when Dad was in high school.

He turns toward Billie and stares her down. "If your sister's not going, neither are you."

He knows I will stay sober and take care of her. He counts on that.

"I don't want to stay in," Billie whines.

"I don't want to go out," I say, setting Dad's empty plate on top of mine and heading for the sink.

"It'll be fun, Teddy Lee," Winston booms from halfway down the hall.

Right. It will be some random party, at some dumpy house at the end of some dead-end road, and Winston will be there, too, even though he's way too old, holding court in the back room and staying to the very end, until the keg sprays air and the easiest girls put out.

I will end up holding Billie's hair while she pukes, or stopping her from getting into a girl fight, and then cap off the night by chasing her down to get her into the car so I can drive home.

If that was fun, then it would be awesome.

Dad is planted in the doorway, the front door resting against his hip, the clock ticking, work waiting.

"Okay . . ." I sigh, knowing this is what he wants, an easy exit, a steady course. "We'll go."

The screen door, the one Winston should have taken down months ago, has already rattled shut behind him.

I'm singing at the top of my lungs, driving down a silent country road. George Michael spills out of me, slipping through the crack in my window and disappearing into the cold dark night.

The very first time I started this car, George was there.

A CD, caught on track number two, was stuck in the stereo when I bought it. So Billie and I listened to "Faith" endlessly, helplessly, day after day, until one brilliant winter morning when she figured out how to pry the CD loose with a nail file. Slip. Pop. We were free!

Billie stashed the file in her purse, and then we twisted and twisted the volume knob, our fingers freezing before the car warmed up in the slant of early-morning sun. Our breath fogged up the windshield faster than the old fan could defrost. The windows finally cleared, but that was it: the stereo was dead.

Billie pounded the dash with her tiny fist and the speakers crackled. Our eyes lit up and then faded as they went silent once more, never to return.

The little knob still turns, and the light comes on, but no sound comes out. It is one of those things you learn to live with, like no phone when the bill goes unpaid, or very limited heat in your house. You put on a sweater. You sing. Even to George Michael, if you have to.

"Faith" is now my go-to singing-alone-while-my-drunk-little-sister-is-passed-out-in-the-seat-next-to-me song. I kind of want to hate it, kind of like I want to hate Billie, but I don't. I can sing my ass off to that song.

I pull into our driveway, my throat hoarse.

I kill the engine, and Billie moans, slumped over in the passenger seat. The seat belt is the only thing holding her up, her legs akimbo, grass stuck to one knee, shoes abandoned. Just one more year of school, I remind myself, and my days of baby-sitting Billie will be behind me.

A light is on in the garage, and the garage door is open. We made just two puke stops on the way home, and still Winston somehow managed to beat us.

I sit and stare at the puffs of breath, or maybe it is smoke, swirling above his head in the cold night air as Billie's breathing settles.

I am tired.

It had been the same party: the same people, the same sad life. Like a film on top of a pond, my life is growing in from the edges, clinging to me, holding me down, stagnant. I can almost smell the duckweed.

Billie snores. There is no need to move her now, so I lean back and let my thoughts tumble and drift.

Loose and light, they lift over the dash and then hover above the garage, escaping the tips of the branches and dancing above the trees before flickering far, far away, farther than the edges of this world, somewhere in the deep dark black where the air becomes the sky and the sky becomes the night.

I am suspended, in the wash that was this Saturday night and the empty Sunday sitting in front of me before Monday morning comes along and we start all over again, safe and simple and routine.

I roll my head along the edge of the seat, staring at the stars.

Suddenly, safety seems overrated.

A chance—to try something new, to see if my music is any good—has opened up, and it is glimmering right in front of me. Dripping down from the Big Dipper and landing in my lap, it is as shiny and big and as bright as the North Star. And I want to jump, to leap, even if all that is below me is dirt.

I lean over Billie to crack the window and then tip her head in its direction, hoping that if she wakes, any barf will roll outward.

The stars sparkle above me as I get out of the car. I am nervous and shaky, but I chalk it up to the temperature. Winter has left Oregon behind and headed north. The early-spring air is cold and sharp, the grass wet under my feet.

Winston is leaning against the old beat-up workbench in the garage. His dark blond hair curls down over his collar. When he sees me coming, his eyes light up brighter than the glow of his cigarette.

I pull a CD from the bottom of my bag—one he hasn't heard before, the one I pushed the buttons for myself—and I set it, silver and shining, on top of the workbench. Winston waits silently, the cigarette drooping from his lips.

"Okay," I say.

I pause, breathing for a second before I commit

completely, because there's no coming back. "I'll do it."

Winston nods.

I reach past him, pull the cap off a thick black felt-tip marker with my teeth, and write across the CD in all caps, "RETURN TO TEDDY LEE."

2

"Teddy!" Winston calls out, trying to get my attention. His voice is muffled even though he is pressing himself up against the thick pane of glass that separates us.

We are in an old recording studio at the radio station. I am standing in the engineer's booth as Winston sets up the studio space for auditions. Dusty cardboard boxes are piled in the corners of the studio, and stacks of white Styrofoam cups tower on a stand next to a burned-out coffeepot, with no coffee.

Winston backs into the far corner of the studio and stands next to a well-used set of drums. I lean closer toward the glass between the studio and the engineer's booth and watch his lips move. "Can you hear me now?"

I shake my head no. It would be great if Winston were

always behind a wall of thick glass. Then I could turn off the sound of his voice with the simple flick of a switch. I sit down on my swively chair, and smile. I like that idea. We should live here.

Winston suddenly straightens up and steps out of the dark corner. A boy is walking into the studio, his jeans sliding low, his T-shirt stretching across broad shoulders. I tilt on my axis toward him.

His dark hair is cropped short, buzzed almost to the scalp, but not quite. He holds drumsticks in his left hand, the ends taped and stars drawn down the length of them in what looks like black Sharpie.

He walks big. In just a couple of steps he is across the dim space and shaking Winston's hand like the real MVP. He isn't as tall as Winston, but nobody is.

On the far side of the glass their arms pump up and down, their voices swallowed by the thick honeycombed walls. My eyes flick back and forth, trying to catch what they are saying.

I am tempted to lean down and hit the button so I can hear every word, but I can't look away long enough to locate the right switch on the console. It is like a cockpit in here: a cockpit covered in cigarette ash and sticky drips of Dr Pepper.

Randy is sitting next to me.

He reaches over, hits the magic button, and says, "Let's hear it, kid."

All business, that guy.

You wouldn't think so with the pooch, the comb-over, and the slightly stoned state of being, but you would be wrong.

I watch as Star Sticks settles in, stretches his hands, and adjusts the stool. He says something I don't catch because I am too busy staring.

His arms are big, but not too big—definitely strong enough to pick me up. I am dying to see what his muscles look like without that shirt. Stupid combed cotton, getting in my way.

He has that line, the one that dark-haired guys get along the cheek and above the jaw when they should have shaved this morning but slept in instead.

His lips make me want to write a love song.

Randy leans over, pushes another button, and then gives the thumbs-up through the glass. He is recording the auditions.

"I'm Ty," the boy says, staring at me through the glass with some seriously amber eyes. He slips a pink sweatband onto his right wrist, watching me the whole time.

"Great," Randy says. "Whenever you're ready."

This Ty is so not my type I am concerned for my sanity. I usually go for the thin, rockery, used- and abused-looking ones, the ones that you can tell right off the bat are no good and a little bit crazy and completely untrustworthy. They are scruffy and scraggly and scented with nicotine, and they never last for long.

I will him to look my way again, try to pull him into my

path, but an explosion of drums pins me to my chair, heavy.

He is tearing through it.

The snare sounds like pistol fire.

His arms rocket—they never seem to stop. His rhythm thumps deep into my chest, replacing my heartbeat. Staccato and steady, each strike hammers all the way down to my toes. I shiver. This guy has staying power.

Winston looks at me with one eyebrow cocked and his arms crossed. He nods and bobs along from his spot along the wall next to the studio door.

Ty is building toward a big finish and I can tell Winston is psyched. His leg jiggles as he scribbles on a legal pad and then presses it up against the glass. "One flyer = one drummer," it says. I smile because Winston isn't always such a whiz at math.

"He's got a heavy foot . . . ," Randy says when the drumming finally stops, "like that Led Zeppelin drummer."

"John Bonham?" I ask.

Randy looks over at me.

"No, no. You know . . . ," he says, shaking his head as if I were the fool here, "the one that drowned in the ocean."

I stare him down, then turn back toward the glass and watch Ty rise up, a white smile breaking out in the middle of his dark sandpaper stubble. Randy, you crazy old man, Bonham choked on his own puke; every Zeppelin fan knows that. And that boy is perfect.

✳ ✳ ✳

Ty does not travel lightly. He showed up at our house this morning with his entire drum kit and two friends in tow. One has shaved hair, like his but not as dark, and a tiny green 7UP T-shirt stretched across his muscles.

His stomach peeks out above his belt as he walks down the driveway. The other one is tall and thin, a gangly redhead.

I didn't know what to expect when Winston told me about the three of them last night. We were walking through the lobby at the station, auditions wrapped, clicking off the lights as we went.

A whole roster of drummers had shown up after Ty, most of them wearing stovepipe jeans and sporting sunken, hairless chests and skinny arms. Not one of them was a girl, and not one of them was any good. We played the recordings back at the end of the day just to be sure.

Winston was pissed; he was hoping for at least one drummer girl to show up and fail miserably so he could console her with cigarettes and wondrous tales of local radio. Honestly, I didn't notice anyone after Ty. He swept all categories: best drummer, best smile, and best muscles. No need for the swimsuit competition. Ty was the one.

Winston said that Ty had been in a band called the Trigger Brothers with three other guys, but it fell apart a year ago when the singer-slash-guitarist ran away, chasing a girl to New York. Now it was just Ty and two other guys.

They've been playing together in someone's basement

ever since, but they aren't anything official. I figure they can play in my garage for now since that is as far as we will probably ever get.

Winston hops up and helps the skinny one with the drum he is carrying. It is bigger around than he is. I stand in the corner of our garage, rocking back and forth on the heels of my boots while they set up, pretending not to be checking out Ty.

Billie is on my left, slowly spinning on a stool that Winston stole from the Dumpster behind the auto parts store. She twirls to the top, stops herself, plays with her phone, and then twirls back down to the bottom, feigning boredom with what is going on around her. Fine by me. Billie can't play an instrument, can't be trusted with brand-new boys or shiny objects, and has a disturbing love of Avril Lavigne. She is only here to watch. But I'm pretty sure she is checking out Ty.

I'm guessing from what Winston told me last night that the one in the soda shirt is Jay. He and Ty seem like brothers, even though they look nothing alike other than the hair. They have the same bounce, the same energy. They finish each other's sentences, each other's jokes. I bet they will be friends forever. Grow up to be gray-haired old men in cardigans and class rings kind of friends.

I move out of the corner to make room for the drum set and lean up against the bench next to Winston. If the other two are half as good as Ty, we are going to get torn up.

Billie twirls until they are set.

Ty counts down, and they crash into it. Some really old rock 'n' roll, then some more complicated and kind of jazzier stuff that could use some horns, and then a few straight-up pop songs that I've heard pounding away in the background at parties and streaming from open car windows at long red lights.

Winston wants us to play classic rock covers since Randy told him that is what bar hoppers want to hear. It seems like these guys can play anything, and that unnerves me. My repertoire is not that big: some classic rock, some favorite singer/songwriter ballads, and the stuff I make up for myself, sitting alone in my bedroom at night.

When they tumble to a stop, Ty looks right at me.

"Do you want to give it a go?" he asks.

I glance over at the redhead.

He has remained silent since they got here. No jokes, no smiling, not a word. He did, however, spend an obsessive amount of time playing scales and warming up.

Ty lifts his chin and says, "We call him Ginger Baker."

"Ginger Baker played the drums," I say.

Dad has a Cream poster tacked up above the washer and dryer at the bottom of our basement stairs. I know Ginger Baker. He is front and center every time I descend with a load of Winston's dirty underwear: sparkly drum kit, sixties Nehru jacket, big hair, and all.

Ty pulls up the sleeves on his worn-out thermal.

"So does he," he says, nodding at Ginger Baker. "Better than me, actually. But he prefers rhythm guitar. I think because it's harder to spell."

I raise an eyebrow at Ginger Baker. He has a lot of hair. Like Mozart, but with freckles.

"He doesn't communicate well," Ty explains. "Needs an interpreter. But he rocks out and can play anything. And he really wants to be in a band."

Jay leans forward and presses his bass against his stomach.

"To get chicks," he stage-whispers.

Ginger Baker winces when Billie giggles and twirls to a stop.

"Are you a matched set then?" I ask. "Or can we get pieces and parts?"

"We're together." Ty answers for all of them. I can tell they talked about it on the way over.

I pause, already intimidated by their unity. It doesn't help that they can also actually play. Why do they want to hook up with a girl and her guitar in a dusty garage way out here where the sidewalk ends?

Winston nudges me with his shoulder.

It doesn't matter to him if I am nervous or intimidated or out of my league. I've always stepped up for him. Helped him out and stayed in the background, holding the flashlight to shine on the never-ending Winston show.

I rolled the newspapers for his first paper route until my

fingers turned black with ink. I returned his one and only jockstrap to the store his freshman year when large turned out to be too large. I lied to countless girls who cried at our door, held the blocks of wood when he learned to karate chop with his bare hands, grabbed the motorcycle before it rolled over him when he dumped his first wheelie. I wrote his book reports and put ice on his black eyes and broken knuckles, and I would do this, too. But not for him: this time I am doing it for me.

I want to know I can do this. I want to be the one to stand in the light.

I straighten up and reach for my guitar.

"Okay," I say.

"Cool," Ty says.

"Cool," Jay repeats, bouncing on his toes, ready to go.

Ginger Baker nods in time to the cadence Ty is quietly rapping onto his thigh. I take that as a yes.

I slide my guitar strap over my shoulder. It is old and worn, covered in the moon and stars, a strung-out constellation of silver and blue thread stitched onto black fabric.

The guitar is old, too. It's my dad's. He used to play weekends in a Cal rock band when he met my mom, before Winston worked his way into this world with that really big head. The Eagles, Poco, mellow stuff that he loves and still hums to this day under his breath while he is tying his boots or putting on his coat and thinks no one is listening.

Ginger's guitar strap has a double helix running down to

his black guitar. Jay's has orange flames that clash with Ginger's hair. My eyes rebound between them, like visual reverb.

We all have mics and amps in front of us. They are kind of old school and definitely used looking, but Winston magically appeared with them this morning, and I did not ask.

I am as ready as I am ever going to get, so I nod.

"Two, three, four. . . ." Ty taps us in.

We play little interludes, bits and pieces of songs, dancing our way through decades of music, jumping around the dial from 30 Seconds to Silversun, seeing how we fit together and where we collide. I tilt my head when I don't know the song, listening hard until I can catch on and catch up.

"How about some vocals?" Winston shouts.

A trail of gray cigarette smoke curls up from his tapping fingers. His right leg rocks along.

I reach up and adjust my microphone. I steady my guitar with shaking hands. The lyrics to the song roll through my mind like a piece of sheet music from an old player piano, but I see only the holes.

I open my mouth to sing, but my voice comes out as a scratch, a scrape, something from the doctor's office that involves a tongue depressor and a pair of rubber gloves. I sound like a cat.

I can feel their eyes meeting up behind my back—especially Ty's. My shoulders curl up. Jay and Ginger Baker stop playing. I feel lost and embarrassed, but Ty keeps his toe tapping, his bass drum thumping along as if nothing ever happened until the boys join back in.

Billie's arm brushes up against mine. She moves in next to me, lifts her chin, and starts to sing. The light coming in through the garage window dances through her hair as she slips right into the song, like she's been ready and waiting to take my place.

When we were in elementary school and my mom was acting parental and responsible for once, she signed me up for an after-school program, two days a week.

I did not want to go, clinging on to her leg, whining and crying and throwing a fit did not want to go.

"I'll go," Billie said. She was waiting then, too.

Off she went every Tuesday and Thursday afternoon, taking my spot. I don't think my mom even bothered to change the name on the registration form.

I'd watch her skip up the walk when she came home, clutching a glitter-covered construction paper chicken or a homemade felt hat with feathers glued on, and seethe with jealousy. She sparkled.

I was jealous of her boldness, her shining blond hair, her ability to breeze away and leave us all behind without a second thought. How could she do that? I couldn't. I stayed home and watched PBS, that awful show with that big red dog. To this day I hate that dog.

"Isn't it scary?" I asked her one night.

She shrugged. "They have a kiddie pool full of rice. We dig in it."

It was that simple for her.

I step back now, hating myself for doing it, and let Billie take my place again. The boys never miss a beat.

It isn't anything particularly spectacular, just a simple Stones song, "Paint It Black," but I can feel all the pieces of the puzzle coming together, snap, click, and there it is, better than good. It is great. Perfect.

Jay ends with a trailing note, and we all look at one another, collective breath held, and then Ty jumps up, knocking over his stool.

"Hell, yeah!" he yells, and Ginger Baker laughs, the first sound I've heard him make.

Winston clamps his lips around his cigarette and claps from the corner. He'd gone out looking for a drummer and ended up with an entire band.

But my heart tightens as Billie squeals and hops around in a tight little circle, the microphone cord wrapping around her legs like a skinny black snake, all while I stand back and watch.

3

Our house is old. A fixer-upper that my parents bought when they first got married that never quite got fixed up. It's dark gray, one story, with white trim and peeling paint on the front door.

The garage is separate from the house: its own little building with a low black roof and a gravel driveway leading up to it. My dad calls the swath of grass between the house and the garage a side yard. He planted a peony bush there way before I was born, and every year we beat a path into that grass walking back and forth across the side yard between the house and the garage.

The peonies bloom in the summer, when the grass is thick and the path almost disappears into the green blades, their sweet scent hanging in the air over the fat, drooping blossoms.

Our yard is flat, and there's no curb out here on the outskirts of town. The street starts where the ragged grass ends and our mailbox sits at the edge, stuck to a post.

I'm standing inside by the side door after Ty and the boys leave that night, waiting and watching while my dad gets ready for work, stubbing my toe against the baseboard and avoiding Billie.

She thinks that saving my ass earlier today in the garage makes her a permanent part of whatever happens next with the band. At first I was surprised when I figured that out.

Then I was mad.

Then I was mad at myself for being surprised.

Why do I think she is ever going to be different?

Why do I keep hoping?

It's always been this way. If I got asked over to a friend's house to play, little Billie came along. If I was going to a party, she was there, waiting for a ride. She borrowed my clothes. Chased after my friends. Copied my hair and my homework. To this day, she takes bites out of my sandwich when she thinks I'm not looking.

There are moments when Billie is good, when I think this is how having a sister is supposed to be, instead of feeling as if I were trapped with a tiny mental patient who escaped from the clinic down the road.

Like the times she leans over and orders into the squawking box at the drive-through when we stop after school. She knows I hate to do it, and she always scores extra dipping sauce or a bonus order of fries, which she holds in her lap, carefully handing me one fry at a time as we fly along toward home.

Or when she tucks down low into my passenger seat, fitting perfectly, her bare feet on the dash, stacking schoolbooks as we swerve into the student lot every morning, digging for a pen in the glove box if we need a note for being late. Not a single employee of our school district has seen my father's signature since Winston started school. Billie has been forging it since she learned cursive writing.

She does excellent harmony, too, never failing to join in— even for "Faith"—though she's sung that one for me a billion times before.

Things like that almost make me forget that she steals and lies and, not too long ago, cost me the only job I've ever had.

I worked after school on Tuesdays and Thursdays and every other Saturday morning last fall at Turner's card shop downtown, selling cards and gifts and little figurines and other stuff that old ladies love.

Lots of husbands dashed in, too, last minute, and bought whatever they could get their hands on. All I had to do was brush my hair and show up with a smile. The crystal vases and poem-filled cards practically sold themselves.

Billie liked to stop by in the late afternoons and lean against the glass cases, spilling the news of the day and leaving fingerprints behind that I would have to clean as soon as she got bored and walked out the door.

Turns out she was walking out the door with a few extra items, too. I honestly didn't know, and I think Mrs. Turner believed my story, but she was unwilling to keep me on anyway.

"I'm so sorry, Teddy Lee," she said.

She told me she wouldn't press charges if Billie and I stayed away. Then she paid me, in cash, before locking the door behind me for the last time late on a cold Thursday night.

Unable to look oncoming traffic in the eye, I slumped behind the wheel of my car all the way home. My little sister was a little thief. Sure, I had always known—there were way too many cheap wristwatches and lollipop wrappers on her dresser to ignore—but now somebody else knew, too.

One of Billie's secrets had spilled outside our house and splattered up onto my shoes. I stepped on the gas and squealed around the corner onto our street.

"Damn it, Billie!" I yelled before the front door had a chance to bounce shut behind me. The living room was empty.

Of course, I thought as I threw my bag into the corner of the couch, why would she be home? It was only a school night.

I pushed our bedroom door open and pulled Billie's secret shoebox out from under her bed. When I tore off the lid, everything inside sparkled in the light of her lamp.

Billie had an entire collection of crystal creatures with Austrian gemlike eyes in there. Big sellers at the shop, they were expensive. She had every single one of them in that box. How hadn't I noticed them trotting out the gift shop door?

I sank down onto the rug, sorting through the tiny paws and cut-crystal manes. At the bottom of the box, wedged between a glass fawn and a glass pony, I found a small pink ballerina, wrapped up in its original tissue.

That last Christmas before she bailed, my mom had given both of us, me and Billie, our own little music boxes. They were cheap dime-store things, made of paste and pressed paperboard covered in a spray of flowers with fake velvety linings.

Billie flipped open the tinny gold latch on hers to reveal a dark purple inside and a blond ballerina twirling to "Send in the Clowns." Mine was pink and played "Tiny Dancer."

My ballerina lasted only a couple of days. The tree was still up and balls of wadded wrapping paper still littered the living room floor when she snapped off at the toes, leaving behind a tiny boinging spring that rotated, dancerless, to mechanical Elton John music and a gold sticker that said MAY CONTAIN LEAD PAINT.

I had wrapped her in Kleenex, whispered a made-up prayer, and laid her to rest in her pink velvet coffin, never to twirl again.

Crossing my legs, I carefully unwrapped the tiny body. I

hadn't seen her for years, not since one morning in middle school when I tossed out everything that reminded me of my mom.

Billie must have dug her out of the trash. I pictured her pawing through the papers and soggy pizza boxes of our life, rifling down, all the way to the bottom to find this buried treasure.

Her ballerina was alive and well, standing in fifth position inside the purple music box next to her bed. It was one of the few things in her life that wasn't broken.

I twirled the pink ballerina on my fingertip, remembering.

Billie trusts me with her secrets. Sure, she steals, she lies, she dips her dirty finger into the sugar bowl every chance she gets, but she also lay next to me, night after night after our mom left, listening to "Tiny Dancer" and reaching over to turn the crank on the back of my music box before the song could end.

I wrapped the little ballerina up again and slid her back into the box and then slid the box back under the bed, safe and sound, protected by dust bunnies and a worn coverlet, storing my anger away for another day.

That day has come. All that anger is boiling away inside me.

A ballerina is one thing—but a band?

My toe shoots out, and I kick the wall instead of stubbing at it. It leaves a mark.

I resent the assumption that I am just going to bring Billie along, that anything I am ever going to do she is automatically a part of, forever and ever, amen.

Especially this. Because an incredible tingling ran through my body the very first time I played. It started in my stomach and made its way out, through every passage and vein and corpuscle, to the very tips of my throbbing fingers.

When I play, I am alive. There is no gray sky. No half-assed attempt. No boring rerun or regurgitated speech or robotic, mindless following of the rules.

Music fits into every empty spot in my brain. It fills it up and makes it swell. I thrum with it. Vibrate with it. Get lost in it.

Billie can barely hold a guitar; forget about learning how to play one. That would require patience and focus and commitment, and she is allergic to all three. She fumbles; she strums; she smiles. The end.

Music has been a single-minded, solitary pursuit that I didn't have to share—until now.

Billie walks past with a bag of chips in her arms as Dad stuffs his keys into his pocket and reaches for his scarf. I hear her crunching toward the couch. The TV turns on, and the sound turns up.

"Maybe it's time to consider putting her to sleep," I say, my eyes following the trail of crumbs she's left behind.

Dad leans down to tighten the laces on his boot.

"She just wants what you have, Ted," he says as he stands back up with a little groan. "She always has."

That is the problem.

I want this time to be different. I want this to be mine.

I want somebody, anybody, to say to me, "It's okay to hate your little sister. Everybody does. It's normal. Expected. She is truly a pain in the ass. We voted, and you are right."

Where is that support group?

How can I sign up for that after-school program?

I'll even bake the cookies.

When it comes to Billie, though, my dad has a blind spot—about the size of the Grand Canyon. He always has. I wish that just this once he would look down into that crevasse and see the river snaking along the bottom, slowly washing me away and cracking the rock. But he doesn't.

Not tonight, with his thoughts glazed over by the many hours of hard work still stacked up in front of him. Bills are piling up; food is running low; the day is disappearing. There will be no arguing with him, no understanding.

He is hardly even here.

I watch him go, his dark boots tromping across the side yard, and feel my heart settling into me, down and deep, resigning like the sun.

"Well," I say to a closed door and a streak of pale peach sky, "I, for one, am tired of it."

✳ ✳ ✳

Winston is throwing a party. I'm not sure what we are celebrating, other than the fact that my dad is working the late shift again and Winston had enough cash to buy a keg.

Maybe we're christening the new band. It has been official for a few hours now, and Jay and Ginger and Ty all have been invited, but so has every other person Winston has ever met and a few new ones he found at the liquor store while picking up the beer.

Last time this happened, we had some dude named Tom living in our house for three weeks. He slept on the couch and cooked excellent scrambled eggs. I taught him how to play "Heart and Soul" on the piano, both parts. He preferred the top half 'cause he didn't have to set his cigarette down to play it.

Tonight our living room is full of Winston's friends. Some of his buddies from the station are here, along with the leftovers from his karate club and most of my high school. Everybody in town knows everybody else, and everyone shows up at the parties. The beer is free, and there isn't anything else to do.

I hate parties. I hate having all these people in my house, in my space, looking at my things and making judgments and pretending that they know something about me because they have seen my stuff.

The boys are always too grabby. The music is always too loud. I usually find myself a spot and stick to it. Watch the craziness from the sidelines and wait to rescue Billie from her latest misadventure.

I take a seat at our piano, facing down a battalion of beer cups sweating white rings onto the wooden top. It is a battered upright that came our way when my grandmother died and my uncles cleaned out her house so they could sell it, quick.

I didn't know my grandmother that well, she wasn't that close to Dad, but she stored some musty music books in the piano bench that opened up like a shallow coffin.

It wasn't exactly in tune when we got it, and the ivory was missing from a couple of the keys, but I could tap out "Heart and Soul" half an hour later. It was a vibratey, slightly cringe-inducing rendition, but somehow my dad hung in there, listening with his head cocked to the side.

Now the keys are sticky with spilled beer. I trace over them, holding my fingers just above the cracked ivory, remembering my mother's favorite song.

She used to open this same piano bench when we visited my grandmother's house. She'd sift through those same books and wrinkled sheet music until she found the exact right one, the only one that she ever played. Then she would sit up perfectly straight, with posture I never saw her use in real life, and start to play.

Her hands were beautiful. She had long, thin fingers with nails that were always shaped and polished, no matter how many hours she worked or how many days she disappeared for.

Billie's hands could be beautiful, too, if she'd stop biting her nails to the stubs and tearing at her cuticles with her teeth. They are a ragged mess, with glitter polish and stick-on decals like unicorns and hearts. It is all dime-store stuff, basically anything small enough to steal.

I have my dad's hands. Kind of squat and stubby; not feminine at all. I keep my nails short.

My mom's rings would glint in the sun as her fingers slid along, swift and true. She played only once or twice a year, maybe, and always just that one song. But she always found the keys without fault, without hesitation. It was magical.

Billie and I would dance around like ballerinas, jumping and twirling and floating through the air with imaginary fairy wings on our backs, instead of worn Fair Isle sweaters and Winston's hand-me-down sweatshirts, dust motes from Grandma's carpet rising into the air to swirl around our arms and our hair while the song filled our heads.

I can play that song by heart.

I hear it in my sleep, memorized it the first week we had the piano.

It is burned into my brain and comes through loud and clear, even now, with the guitars crashing in from the borrowed black speakers on my left and the game of Three Man rattling over in the corner.

My fingers slide silently over the keys, note by note, as I lose myself in my memories.

"What is that all about?"

Ty nods down at my hands, and my face flushes as his fingers move in next to mine, hovering over the keys as if we were playing a duet.

A dull roar comes up from the couch behind us. Jay has rolled doubles, and now someone else has to drink. Ginger watches the action from the corner of the couch: a sentinel.

"Nothing," I say, shaking the last few notes from my mind.

"That," he says, scooting me over on the worn bench with his hip as he stretches his hands across an octave each, "did not look like nothing."

His knuckles are banged up. He smells clean, like soap.

"It looked"—he glances at me with a raised eyebrow and plays a low chord—"heavy."

He leans in and moves eight keys up the piano and says, "Complicated."

His arm reaches across mine, honing in on one last chord, high and light, and says, softly, "Bittersweet."

The word hangs in the inch of air between us.

"Show me," he says, his hands next to mine.

I shrug and let my hands land in my lap. How did he find me here—past the people and the party and the chaotic jumble of mismatched furniture? Was he looking? And how did he know exactly how I was feeling? My fingers had hovered over the keys for only a few seconds, but somehow he had seen it all. I slump away from him, staring across the room.

Billie is threading her way through the crowd. The fingers

of some boy are hooked around her pinkie as she pulls him along, her eyes sloshing full. When she staggers, the boy slides closer.

His arms wrap around her tight. A bit too tight for some boy she most likely met while buying a pack of cigarettes, probably just yesterday. Now I bet they are beyond best friends.

Some kids pick up stray dogs. Billie picks up stray people.

They become very territorial and protective, not realizing that in a short time she will become distracted or bored and move on, leaving them alone and lonely, until she runs into them in a parking lot somewhere and invites them to Thanksgiving dinner. They are usually stupid enough to show up. We have weird Thanksgivings. We have weird everything.

Ty watches me watching Billie.

"Why don't you have a boyfriend?" he asks, pressing his shoulder, warm, against mine.

The room squeezes in small and tight when he speaks, the crowd around us disappearing, a blur of color and light in the periphery of my vision, unnecessary detail.

'Cause you haven't asked me out yet.

That's what Billie would say. Then she would probably rest her hand on his package. But I can't say that. I could never do that. I'm not like Billie. Boys don't run into me in parking lots or bump up against me on piano benches. Tonight is turning out to be an exception.

I look back at Ty. His cheeks are flushed from the beer or

the warmth of the room. They glow at me, lulling and pulling me in, inviting me to reach over and touch them, to lay my cool palms flat against their heat.

My eyes dance along the edge of the keyboard. I wish it were true: that Ty really is interested, that he wants to know the answer and me. I steady myself, finding my breath and focusing in on middle C.

"Tell me," he says, nudging my shoulder.

" 'Cause nobody ever asked," I answer.

My heart races when Ty's eyebrows lift and his lips spread into a smile that puts all other boys to shame.

He rocks away from me, pressing his fingers into the keys.

Then he rocks back.

"Until now," he says.

He rocks away again and I move with him, swaying on the bench as his hands ascend and descend, playing a song for me, soft and low.

4

Most time the notes and music and words are far away, drifting along, slightly out of my reach. They are there, but I can't get to them. They tease me for another time.

But in other moments, like right now—with my head full of Ty, his voice, his smell, the soft parts inside me still rocking to the rhythm he set out for us seven nights ago—they are so present and clear they practically write themselves. I find it strange and amazing. Where do they come from? How do I know which words will fit? Why do the words always match the melody so perfectly?

I have little control over it. I just try to keep up, the blue lines of my notebook holding me together, straight and orderly, safe and sane, as I fill it with scribbles that I hope I can read later when the rush has passed. I press so hard with my pen that I can feel the words on the other side of the page. It is so loud I don't even have time to think.

I don't know how to write the actual music part, with the bars and the clefs and all that, but I have worked out a system.

I keep the melodies in my head and write clues down next to the lyrics so I can remember them later. Like, this is the one that sounds like a wet winter morning, or this is the one that bounces like a baby's curls in a stroller.

Not bad, considering I started out with nothing but a stolen guitar, a used piano, and a book borrowed from a rolling library. That book is the source of all my knowledge, and I have never once thought about returning it. The fine for it is probably worth way more than our house by now.

My mom loved the bookmobile. Oh, she wouldn't go in, she said it made her claustrophobic; but we had the schedule taped to the front of the fridge, and every two weeks, like clockwork, we packed our Marlboro Lights canvas bag full of dog-eared books and marched the however many blocks to where the RV was parked.

She would stand on the curb and smoke while Billie and I climbed the three steps into the curved cab. My mom couldn't commit to more than a magazine at a time but always said to us, "It's important to have a love of the printed word." One of her English teachers must have told her that once.

Plus, the bookmobile was free. She didn't even have to scratch under the couch cushions for change to take us there. I had read almost everything in the children's section by the time she disappeared in the second grade. All the good stuff anyway.

"Do you have any books on guitars?" I asked the librarian one morning.

She handed me a worn board book without looking at me. It had a chicken on the cover pecking at a guitar string.

I held the chubby pages in my hand, disgusted.

"No," I said, "how to play the guitar."

"I have one," she said, finally seeing me, "but it's for grown-ups."

"Can I check it out anyway?" I asked.

"Is your mom or dad here, honey?"

I lifted my hand to point out the window to where my mom usually was, flicking ashes at her ankles while Mr. Conway chatted her up in his plaid golf shorts, but there was only a yellow street sign: SPEED HUMP.

"She's waiting in the car." I lied, my eyes honest and big.

"Okay, then."

She smiled at me as she took my card, probably more than happy to find someone reading above her grade level in the tiny library on wheels.

I cracked the spine as Billie and I walked back home. Apparently not many adults in town were learning *How to Play* the *Guitar in 25 Easy Lessons*. The ink inside was still fresh and strong.

Glancing up from the complicated finger diagrams as we walked along, I wondered: How did you end up being the librarian in the bookmobile? Instead of the one manning the reference desk or, you know, being in charge of the Dewey Decimal System? Was there a hierarchy?

Was she the only one with a valid driver's license and the ability to parallel park a thirty-five-foot vehicle alongside the curb? Or did she just draw the short straw, mumbling a blue streak of big, encyclopedic bad words under her breath when her turn came?

I hopped off the curb and hoped not. I was glad for her. She let me have a grown-up book and I was going to learn to play the guitar, all by myself, one easy lesson at a time.

From the very beginning—all the way back to page one, "How to Hold Your Instrument"—the guitar was perfect for me. It was clean and sharp. The lessons were systematic and structured. The next steps were laid out for me in black and white, and the ones after that, too. I knew exactly where to go.

Pressing its solid body against my softness, I studied and struggled and wished hard, tripping along chord after chord, finding a place to hide, to live, to feel safe, lost in the notes and strumming.

During the dark nights and the long days after our mom left us, it soothed me. It grounded me. I could not float away in a bad dream or drift away, forsaken, while it was in my hands.

I learned enough to play Billie to sleep, my little fingers rasping along the strings in our lamp-lit room until she snored.

"Go to sleep now," Dad would whisper when he walked into our room and found me awake. He would lean the guitar up against my bed as I snuggled down and closed my eyes, protected under its silvery moon and stars.

I don't play Billie to sleep anymore, but I still stay up late, writing down my words, building them into songs by the light of that same lamp.

My head has been crazy all week, crammed full and bursting with songs about Ty. It's been seven days since we swayed together on that piano bench, held fast by a low vibration only the two of us could feel, and I can barely keep up. It's as if he turned everything I had inside me up to ten.

But he doesn't call. He doesn't text. He simply shows up for practice every night, smiles hello, and then beats his drums behind me.

I have been filling the margin of my notebook with song titles like:

"Show Me"

"Tell Me"

"Rockin"

"Boys Suck Big Time"

"Ask Me Out Already"

And, my favorite:

"My Beautiful Disaster"

I take my pen and scribble a line through them all. They aren't right. They are small and short and don't capture how I feel, how I have wished for just a word from him, any word, how I have been waiting for the night to fall, over and over all week long.

Because that's when they appear—three black silhouettes against the orange light of evening as my heart stretches out, eyes reaching down the driveway for the second one in line. Jay bounces in first, and Ginger stands tall, bringing up the rear. Ty is the glue.

How I breathe when I see him. Dance inside when he smiles at me.

Ty has a routine, the same steps every night. He adjusts his stool, tightens the cymbals, stretches his hands. He touches the edge of the snare and then sits down, facing me.

Caught, I look away as fast as I can.

His fingers move along to the music when he is listening to Jay or Ginger play. When he thinks nobody is looking.

I write about how hard it was raining last night and how I hurried to open the side door as they rushed in, Jay and Ginger through the garage door. Ty through the side door I was holding open.

He ducked in and brushed his hand up against mine as he passed.

"I know what you're thinking," he said. "Late again . . ."

But, you smell so good was my only thought as I stood frozen with the doorknob in my hand. I want to eat him up with a tiny spoon so he lasts forever.

Flipping the page in my notebook, I rush from one night into the next, one song into the next, feeling the dark ink from my pen smearing onto the soft curve of my left hand as I put it all onto paper.

"This is the one where the stars shine just for me," I write next to the song about how I study the drumsticks Ty leaves behind every night, waiting for him.

How the stars are worn gray from his hands.

How I don't dare sit or hold them in my hands.

How he isn't mine . . . yet.

5

"Don't smoke in here tonight," Winston announces as he walks into the garage, snapping me awake. I am tired. I stayed up too late last night writing songs about Ty and it's finally catching up with me.

A waxy bag of little powdered donuts is crooked in Winston's left arm. He eats each one in a single bite. No muss, no fuss. They disappear, swallowed whole, in what can only be a wet, sharp death.

"I am afraid the place might blow up."

He gestures toward a stack of dented metal cans in the corner, half covered by a dark green tarp, that wasn't there the night before. I don't ask where they came from or how big the explosion will be. Sometimes it is better not to know the details.

I don't know why he feels the need to announce our new smoke-free environment. He is the only one who smokes. Jay pretends to, and Billie tries once in a while; but she is just an amateur. She mostly carries a pack around so she will have something to fill up her purse. Lord knows there is never any cash in there.

Knowing his fear of flames is completely justified, I nod at Winston anyway.

I've seen him try to light a cigarette with one of the gas burners in our kitchen and singe off most of his left eyebrow. Billie got him a lighter that Christmas to keep him intact. (Stole him a lighter, I should say.)

He keeps it crammed in his front pocket, along with this psycho blue rabbit's foot key chain Mom won for him at the fair. It is so old the rabbit's foot is almost bald. It is more like a knuckle.

He started our couch on fire once a few years ago, too. It was a hot summer night, and Billie and I were outside catching fireflies in a Mason jar. Billie liked to crush their bodies and smear the glowing guts across her cheeks like war paint.

I looked up from her face, glittering in the deep blue dusk, to see a stream of smoke rolling out of our open living room window.

"Dad! Dad!" I screamed, and he rushed out of the garage, the side door banging shut behind him.

I pointed at the gray swirl drifting out of the living room

window, and he disappeared in a flash, a string of swearwords trailing behind him into the house. My heart beat like a tom-tom, preparing for homelessness.

Billie continued to dance around the yard, arms out, the streaks on her cheeks fading as the sun sank behind the trees and our front yard filled with smoke.

Winston had fallen asleep on the couch, his cigarette blazing a hole beneath him.

We lived with the big burned smoke hole in the corner of our couch for years. My dad just kept adjusting the cushions and propping a limp pillow into the corner to hide it.

We finally got a new sofa when my grandma died. It came with the piano. It was still just like new since it had been covered in plastic the entire time she owned it. We pulled that plastic off and Winston carted the old, burned beauty to the dump with a smile, his firebug days safely behind him.

Jay and Ty were warming up when Winston walked in, and Jay is still playing a note on his bass that bounces enough to make your back teeth rattle.

Winston sets the bag of donuts onto the closest speaker and wipes his fingers onto his jeans.

"Take the edge off the heavy." He winces at Jay.

Jay stops the sharp, grinding note and spins, switching songs on the fly.

He is so fast. I study his shoes and his fingers, wondering how either one holds up.

He bobs his head at Ty, and the beat changes behind me, becoming low and deep and addictive. I want to drown in it. Throw my arms open wide and fall back, because I know Ty's low, solid beat will be there to hold me up.

He backed me up when everyone else dropped off that first day in the garage. He waited for me later that night at the piano.

He keeps holding on, as if he knows there is more to see and he is willing to wait for it. "It'll be worth it," I'll say as I dance along on the high notes above him, showing him what I've got.

He's only a few feet away, but like always, there's too much music and too many people in my way.

The fluorescent tube hanging above Ty's head flickers, momentarily lighting up his dark hair. I imagine feeling it, sharp and prickly one way, soft and slippery the other, as it buzzes along under my fingers while he leans in and finds my neck, his lips warm and soft.

Blood rushes toward every exit point—my toes, my ears, the tip of my tongue—and I take a step closer to him.

My guitar cord has been getting shorter and shorter as I slowly move myself toward him. I am tightening up our already tiny garage, day after day, practice after practice, inch by inch, waiting for the moment, again, when it will just be the two of us.

I join into the song Ty and Jay are playing and take a step

closer still. Now only a pile of tires stacked up in the corner, a half-built but completely forgotten engine, some potentially explosive cans, and a few primed car panels are between us. I tiptoe even closer.

At this rate I will be standing on the edge of his snare drum by the end of the night.

We play through the songs we all know by heart and some trickier B sides that none of us have heard before. Winston copied the sheet music for us down at the station and then returned the books to the music store for a full refund.

Ginger and I don't read along. He closes his eyes and plays as if every song already existed inside his head, just press play. I have to listen until I can find my place; then I can drop in and feel it.

I am studying my fingers, figuring out an unfamiliar hook when everyone else stops playing. I look up and blush, the singular sound of my guitar filling the air.

"We have an exam tomorrow," Jay says, nodding toward Ginger Baker. "Gotta get ready."

Jay and Ginger start sliding their guitars into their cases and snapping the latches shut, but Ty stays put, planted behind his drum set.

Maybe he doesn't have the same test, I think as I pull my guitar strap over my head and prop my guitar against the stool next to me. I'm not sure how their fancy school works. They probably don't just squish everyone together based on size and then crush their spirits, like they do at mine.

The former Trigger Brothers all go to Walden. It sounds completely crunchy, but it is actually a school for those on the fringes. For kids who are too smart or too scary or too special for regular, boring, public education.

I picture a combo of geniuses and socially frustrated misfits studying together and bouncing into each other in the hallways that are painted with happy murals and construction paper silhouettes of Einstein and Brahms.

Where fighters and biters and firestarters are mixed in with the truly exceptional. Sort of like, this guy can play Beethoven's Symphony No. 9 by ear, and this guy can sit in the corner and knock on a wooden block while drooling. Welcome to the sixth grade!

Jay told me that he and Ty and Ginger have been there since they turned eleven.

I can tell that Jay makes it through on charm and superior mechanical abilities. He wired one of the older amps back into service and put a dimmer switch on the light just inside our garage door before the end of our second day together. He says it enhances the mood.

But Ty and Ginger are total goners. Gifted is what teachers usually call it, though. It sounds better that way.

The garage door is open, and I can hear the sounds of dishes being done and TVs turning on down the street. It is starting to get dark, and lamps are lighting up as kids run home, that last game of horse played out.

Jay checks his phone and pulls the cord on his bass. It snaps out of the amp and slides across the floor.

Winston and Billie left for cigarettes long ago. They won't be coming back anytime soon. One time Winston went out for a pack and called two days later, from Michigan.

Jay reaches over and adjusts the mood lighting to soft and romantic.

Ty shrugs and sets his sticks on top of his snare.

Jay and Ginger walk a few feet down the driveway to Jay's car: wingmen with guitar cases bumping up against their hips. They stop and wave good-bye: a short muscular arm and a tall, freckly salute.

I wave and bend over before Ty can look at me. We are so set up.

"I hope they work out," I hear Jay say with a low laugh, "'cause I'm not hauling that drum kit back out of there."

I straighten up from locking my guitar into its case and smooth out the front of my shirt. My fingers are shaky. It is finally, nerve-wrackingly—have my armpits always been this sweaty?— just Ty and me.

I am used to helping Billie and Winston get what they want, but I don't know what to do when everyone else is helping me. Should I act surprised or nervous or embarrassed, or just run right over there and hop on top of him?

I feel naked standing here without my guitar.

Ty stops pretending to be tightening down a cymbal.

"Give me a ride home?" he asks.

"Sure," I say. "Let me get my keys."

No hopping necessary.

The sun is sliding low, the sky fading from lavender to black when I climb behind the wheel of my car and pop the lock on the passenger door for Ty. It sticks sometimes.

It had been hard to find a car that had enough properly working parts to pass the inspection before my driving test. I had to borrow our neighbor's minivan; Dad's passenger taillight got knocked out one night when Winston was chased by a jealous boyfriend. It's a good thing he didn't knock up Mr. Tenny's daughter, or I never would have gotten my license.

I bought my own car as soon as I could, and I let Winston drive it as little as possible. He is too libidinous.

Ty and I drive in total silence for a while, more than a couple of blocks, making our way around the edge of town.

"Ginger likes Titchy," he says out of the blue, pointing me to the right at the next intersection.

"Who's Titchy?" I ask.

For a second I think maybe Ginger Baker is in love with a cat.

He shakes his head and laughs. "For a band name."

"Oh." I take the next left, following his finger again.

"But we're not British," I say. "Although Ginger Baker

does kind of look like a young king of England."

"Twitch then?" he suggests as the houses get bigger and the yards start to slope and grow.

"And definitely not punk." I wince.

Ty sits, no tapping, his hands calm in his lap for once, and looks at me out of the corner of his eye.

"Wait," I say, looping back to the beginning of the conversation as we stop at a red light. "Ginger said that?"

"Yes."

"I mean—and this is a weird question to have to ask—he speaks?"

"All the time." Ty laughs. "He's just very selective."

"Should I be offended?"

"Hope not."

He looks over at me like he is wondering if I have the hots for Ginger Baker. I shake my head. I so do not.

Ty points straight ahead, and we pull into a quiet neighborhood under a canopy of tall, curving trees. A leafy arch of sabers stands over the wide street, and I feel protected as we pass underneath, my crooked headlights leading the way.

Happy people live here, I think. Happy families that eat prime rib and grow organic gardens and have perfect teeth.

"I was thinking . . . ," I say, slowing to look both ways at an unmarked intersection, studying the striped lines of the crosswalk that separate safety from danger.

Ty waits for me to finish my sentence.

I breathe out before I press on the gas because I have been thinking about a band name for so long and have never said it out loud to anyone else before, but here it goes. "Red Velvet Crush."

It sounds better now than it ever did in my head.

Ty leans his elbow up against the door and rests his chin down, staring out his window, taking my idea in, and giving it some gravity.

"Cool," he finally says.

Thank God.

He directs me toward the third house on the right. "It reminds me of cars."

"And cake," I add, because cake is always a bonus. Always.

We pass his driveway and pull up in front of his house.

"Perfect."

I'm not sure if he is commenting on my choice for a band name or my superior parking ability. I learned from Winston, who can drive better with his knee while rolling a joint than most people can with their hands at ten and two. Either way, I am good.

He doesn't get out.

I don't really breathe.

Instead Ty reaches down and pulls a CD from the side pocket of my passenger door. George Michael smolders back at me. Crap.

"Really?" he asks, incredulous.

He sets the CD flat onto his palm, as if it were poisonous, and opens it up. It creaks like a vault or a crypt.

I know the case is cracked. But still, I watch as the cover falls off and the CD rolls down his leg and onto the floor.

So much for this love affair.

"What can I say?" I shrug as he bends down to pick up the pieces. "It came with the car."

It's true.

"I know what you need," Ty says.

"Oh, really?"

"Yes, really."

He snaps the corner back onto the front cover and slides the whole case back into the door. Then he dusts his hands off on his jeans, as though attempting to wipe away the shame of the eighties, and turns toward me.

"Come with me?" he asks, his eyes warm and steady on mine.

A million heartbeats in one second can't be wrong. I put the car into park.

Lit only by porch light, we make our way across the soft, grassy rise of Ty's front yard. The dark wood shingles and tall, pitched roof of his house wait for us in dusky stillness.

He opens the front door and turns on the hall light. I step in behind him. It smells clean inside, but unused. Like everything is brand-new and nothing has ever been accidentally set on fire.

Ty kicks off his shoes and bounces down a set of stairs at the end of the hall, his frame loose and jangly.

I kick mine off, too, and try to keep up, but I am busy staring at everything. Taking it all in.

A baby grand piano gleams under the windows facing the street in the front room. A blue glass bowl sits on top of a sideboard, next to a stack of *National Geographics*. I touch the edge of the bowl as I pass by. The glass is smooth and cool under my fingers.

Lining the stairs is a series of photos—Ty's school pictures—one from every year. He grows up with each step. His schoolboy hair gets bigger, then rockabilly, then punk, then metal and screamo. I laugh and start again at the top, watching his smile go from gapped to big and toothy to a Crest commercial.

The last one, his senior picture, is straight-edge Ty. Shaved short, he smiles back at me with perfect teeth. The same smile looks up at me from the bottom step, waiting.

"Where are your parents?" I ask in a shy voice I didn't even know I owned. I step down to him.

"Book club," he says, and takes my hand, pulling me across a sea of thick carpeting that swallows me up to my ankles.

I am impressed, by the answer and by the room, where everything is soft and subtle, in shades of tan, like living inside a warm cup of coffee. But Ty keeps going.

"Farmers market?" He leads me to an entire wall lined with books and record albums, obviously just guessing.

"At this hour?" I ask, playing along.

"It's special." He kneels down, flipping through the albums on the bottom shelf. "Nightshades only."

He looks over his shoulder at me.

Grinning, he gives it one more try. "Turkish prison?"

He must be used to being alone in this big house. I honestly can't remember being alone in my house. Ever. With Billie around I barely get to use the bathroom on my own. She busts in while I am in the bathtub.

"Take these." Ty slides albums out across the carpet toward my toes, one after the other: Lissie, London Grammar, The Runaways.

"But this—" Ty says when he finally stops flipping and stands up.

He taps the album cover with his finger. "This is what you need."

"Carole King?" I ask, spying the cover as he walks over to a stereo. It is sleek and expensive looking.

"History," he says.

He lifts the record player's slender arm and slides the album onto a shiny silver post. The record drops silently, like magic, and the arm moves over it, hovering for a second before it lowers, filling the room with pure, melancholy piano music.

The song strikes a chord deep in my chest, somber and heavy, reminding me of my mom. I swallow hard, afraid of falling into a place that is dark and jagged and full of crags, fighting to stay here, where it is warm and safe, lit by the softest of bulbs.

Ty turns toward me and nods along. A mellow drumbeat is coming in through the speakers hidden in the ceiling, thumping low and deep.

"Nice offer," I say as he steps over the albums scattered across the floor and moves toward me. "But we don't have a record player."

He does not look disappointed. "Then I guess you'll have to come back."

He holds his arms out, and I step into them, sinking farther into the carpet. His heart is beating, muffled and warm, as we start to dance. We aren't really even dancing, just holding each other, circling. His body is close against mine. I smell the sweetness of his neck and his shoulder. His hand rubs across my lower back slowly, softly, perfectly, melting me to him.

I reach up and run my hand along the back of Ty's head, his hair buzzing under my fingertips. It is soft and prickly.

I sneak in under the bridge of his nose. "I'm skipping ahead," I say, and I kiss him.

His lips are warm and soft and start breaking into a smile as soon as I stop. He breathes out in a rush of warm air that mingles with mine, and I lean back in for more. Up close, his eyes have flecks of gold in them.

My bare feet touch against his tube-socked toes as one song spins into the next and the next and the next until the album ends and there is nothing but us, hearts beating fast, surrounded by a soft, sweet hiss.

I can't wait for next time.

Ty pulls up to my house on Saturday morning behind the wheel of a champagne-colored minivan. It has a "My Son's an Honor Student at WA" bumper sticker on the back and squishy-looking tires with whitewalls. It is all very street legal and suburban looking.

I step off the front porch and walk across the yard.

"Are we going to play soccer?" I ask as Ty makes his way around the front of the van and reaches for the passenger door.

"It's my mom's," he says as he pulls the door open for me.

I duck in under his arm. It's been two nights since we danced in his basement, and I am still sleeping in the shirt that pressed up against him, his smell slowly fading in a nightly battle against my flowered sheets and fabric softener.

I breathe him in deep as I climb into the car. Ahhh . . . there's nothing like the real thing.

Ty swings my door shut and then jogs back around the front as I check out the van.

The interior is boring beige with stripes of corporate tan.

Spare change is lined up by denomination in the appropriate slots, although there seems to be an abundance of pennies. It smells great inside, but that might just be Ty.

He starts the engine and swings out into the street.

"Where's Billie?" he asks as I click my seat belt.

"Still sleeping."

For once Billie's sleepiness has worked in my favor. Usually it just makes me late for school.

"And Winston?" Ty asks, steering around the pile of broken blinkers and headlights at the end of our street. It is a tricky left.

I lean forward, looking to the right along with him.

"Slumped on the couch, smoking cigarettes and watching cooking shows."

He looks at me as if that requires further explanation.

"It's what he does when we're low on groceries."

Ty avoids the slow, lazy curves of the suburbs and heads toward downtown. He drives with his left leg bent and leaning up against the door.

"Where are we going?" I ask.

"I want to show you something."

"What?" I am not good at surprises. Not since the second grade anyway.

"Well . . ." he says. "It's someplace, actually." He checks over his shoulder to switch lanes. "I kind of live there. I think you're going to like it."

"How do you know?"

"I just know," he says.

I remember the dancing and the albums he picked out the other night. How he pulled the word bittersweet out of the air as we sat at the piano. I cross my fingers and tuck them under my leg. He's been right so far.

We drive until we are kind of downtown, but not really. The tall glass offices and department stores are still blocks away. Low brick buildings and shops surround us with handmade signs inviting us to SHOP LOCAL.

Ty drives down an alley, turns right, and then parks the minivan in a spot on the corner.

"Rock star parking," he says, lining the van up with the curb.

I lean over to look out his window. It counts as rock star parking only if we are right outside where we want to be. The storefront on his side of the street is jam-packed with banjos and ukuleles. The window gleams, glass and wood bodies and metal strings. Silver fittings and fingerboards sparkle in the morning sun.

"You live at The Wall of Sound?" I ask.

"Just wait," Ty says, opening his door. "In a minute you're going to wish you did."

I climb out. Hey, if they have an empty bed and are willing to turn the heat past sixty-five degrees in the winter, I might consider it.

A bell jingles above the door when we walk in.

"Ty!" the man behind the counter says as soon as the door swings open. We are the only customers. The man has dark, poofy shoulder-length hair and a drooping mustache.

"Tony!" Ty grins and walks toward the counter.

They shake hands, and I look around. A wall of guitars is in front of me, a wall of brass is on my left, and the entire back room seems to be devoted to drums. Pianos are planted wherever there is room.

Wood gleams like gold honey.

Metallic strings flicker in the sun.

Polished silver keys and pedals sparkle.

I spin and take it all in again. I take a step, change my mind, and step the other way. What should I touch first?

Thank God Billie isn't here. She would break something.

I walk toward the wall of guitars, picking out the one I would want if I could afford a new guitar. Guitars of every color hang on that wall. Bright yellow ones, shiny apple red ones, matte black death metal ones, even pinstriped flying Vs straight from 1984.

"What do you think, Teddy Lee?" Ty calls out.

I have never heard him say my name before, and it stops me in my tracks. I immediately decide he should add it to the end of every sentence.

The price of postage went up again, Teddy Lee.

Dracula was Bram Stoker's most popular book, Teddy Lee.

The sun rises and sets for you, Teddy Lee.

"Now I see why it's called The Wall of Sound," I say, knowing that it's stupid, that everybody probably says that. But I can't help it. I am having a hard time not hopping around on my tippy toes with my eyes wide and my mouth in a little O. It's possible I might need defibrillation.

Tony laughs and says, "I do my best."

"I told you you'd like it," Ty says, leaving the counter.

He was right. It is amazing.

Ty walks past me. "First things first," he says, holding his hands out behind his back, reaching for mine. I hesitate, then grab for them. He leads me over toward the windows and a black baby grand in the corner.

Tony follows us, dusting his fingers along drum tops and piano lids as he goes. I am jealous; he can touch everything.

"You play, right?" Ty asks as he sits me down on the black bench.

"I do."

I wait for him to sit at the drum set next to me. It is pearly gray, like the sky before a storm. Instead he walks back over to the wall of guitars with Tony.

Of course he plays the guitar. He probably plays everything, including the glockenspiel.

"What about that one?" Ty asks, pointing toward a neon green Mustang.

Tony shakes his head. "Not today," he says. "Too much flash."

I agree, even though they haven't asked for my opinion.

Tony moves two guitars over and one guitar up. Ty nods, and Tony takes down a custom-built acoustic guitar, all black with a silver spiderweb painted on the body. He hands it to Ty.

"More your style," he says.

Ty tunes it, his head tilted.

There is no strap; he holds the guitar propped against his hip. I stare at his arms, picturing the muscles flexing under his Henley.

He walks toward me and starts to strum.

I raise my hands over the piano keys, my fingers wobbly because he has never actually heard me play and because Tony is watching.

"Death Cab?" Ty asks.

I shake my head.

"Teen Spirit?"

"Definitely not."

"Sublime?" He pauses. "Come on . . . everybody loves some Sublime."

"Yeah, everyone forty-five and over," I say. "Besides, that's stoner music."

He stops strumming. "Do you have something against stoners?"

"Not strictly speaking," I say. Lord knows I've spent enough time with them.

Ty runs his fingers along the strings, thinking.

"I know," he says. He nods like he's had the best idea ever. "'Yesterday.'"

Yesterday? Nothing happened yesterday. It was two days ago I kissed you, I think.

He starts in on the first few notes of the song "Yesterday," and I freeze.

My hands plunk onto the keys. "You're kidding, right?"

Ty stops, too.

"Wait . . . you don't like the Beatles?" he asks, looking suspiciously at Tony.

"Nope," I say, and Tony bounds toward me. He leans against the side of the black piano and reaches down. My hands are shaking for real now. I don't know what to expect.

"Well then," Tony says, catching up my right hand into a tight, warm squeeze, "welcome to a small and very exclusive club."

"Happy to be here," I say, relieved.

My reflection smiles back at me from the glossy piano top.

Ty stands in the middle of the room and sighs. "I can't believe I've found the two people in the world that don't like the Beatles."

"Believe," I say, and play a series of twinkling, totally Lennonish notes.

Tony laughs and starts walking back to the counter. "Now *that* sounds like a Beatles song."

"Okay," Ty says. "Pick something else. Your choice."

He steps closer to the piano and rests the guitar against his hip again, waiting for me. I tuck my hair behind my ears and sit up straight.

"Ready?" he asks.

"This is weird," I say, looking at him.

Ty shakes his head. "It's cool, I play here all the time."

"No . . ." I say. "It's just that I never see you standing up. It's weird."

I swear I can hear Tony chuckling behind the counter.

"Just play," Ty says.

So I do. I kick into it, hard and fast, playing the song we danced to in his basement, but live and much louder. I have been practicing it at home every chance I get, remembering how it felt to be close to him for the first time, how my heart drubbed down into my toes, how my hands rested on him, light and new.

I work the pedals on the baby grand, feeling all the notes, full steam ahead.

I don't slow down, or ease into it, or even give Ty a chance to catch up to me, but somehow he does.

6

Jay and Ginger are in for it. I can tell by the way they stand straighter and stare whenever Billie walks into the garage for practice. Today their mouths hang open, and Jay's bass swings low and loose, temporarily forgotten.

I've seen it before. It is a side effect of her bounciness, her indifference, and the little space between her front teeth. Boys love Billie.

But Ty never even seems to notice her. He is either very well behaved or impervious to her charms. Maybe he is still hypnotized, spinning under the dazzling spell of The Wall of Sound and its sea of shining instruments.

I am still feeling it, too, and returning to the dusty dimness of the garage is a bit of a disappointment. But Jay and Ginger are here when we pull up, spilling stupid jokes and guitar licks out into the street, and sliding under the moon and stars strap feels like home. It sparkles when the light hits it just right.

Billie is sporting a fresh scrape on her knee. It looks suspiciously like rug burn, but Billie always has a bruise or a scratch or a bump. A nick. A little something that she picks up during the day and has no idea how it happened.

She bumps along with a smile on her face, knocking into everyday shit, unknowingly changing the trajectory of everything around her. Lives, furniture, even things that appear to be set in stone are nudged into another dimension when she bounces up against them: poor, unprepared world.

Her eyes follow mine from her knee to her face, where they flicker and hold, seemingly abashed, but I bet I just imagine that.

What was she up to while Ty and I were out?

I tell myself she tripped.

Ty waits for her while she gets set, tapping out the intro to the next song on the rim of his snare. Jay joins in, and Ginger Baker rolls his head back and forth to the beat, already lost.

When Ginger goes to bed at night, I bet musical notes dance before his eyes, while bosomy girls in satin nighties thread in and out of staves, weaving themselves into his unwritten masterpieces.

Billie starts singing, and soon she is screwing everything up. I know it's on purpose because songs she has known her whole life are coming out wrong. "Wish" becomes "kiss." "Boys" becomes "noise."

There is no excuse. Growing up with Winston was a lifelong primer in classic rock. We skipped right over "The Farmer in the Dell" and went straight on to "Black Dog," drifting along on a constant stream of acoustic intros and cigarette smoke.

The periodic table and the parsing of sentences fall right through Billie's brain, but those lyrics are stuck in her head, like bubble gum on the bottom of her boot. This has to be payback for spending the day with Ty.

I scowl at her from behind my guitar and wonder what will come next.

Finally Jay jumps forward and whispers over her shoulder. "Ah . . . it's 'repent,' " he says, "not 'red pants.' "

Billie turns to look at him, eyebrows arched.

Jay ducks his chin and slides back into his spot, lining his worn Vans up behind his microphone, completely apologetic and still slightly goggled by her presence.

"'Sokay." She smiles sweetly, finally swimming in the attention she was after.

We find our places again while Billie sways, waiting for the start of the next verse.

She stands, hand on her skinny hip, the fake fur trim surrounding the hood on her parka tangled into her hair. As the music starts building, she arches toward the mic, and I watch her transformation from little sister to rock star. It never fails to impress me, even under the dull fluorescent tubes of our garage.

Her five feet two inches stretch, suddenly seeming much bigger than her usual scabbed-up little self. A rasp rattles into her voice, husky and low, summoning up a southern accent that hasn't existed since the end of the Confederacy. Then a sound, huge, rocks from that tiny body.

I stare at her in amazement, remembering her dressing Barbie dolls and eating her breakfast cereal with milk that was definitely well past sour but not quite chunky, and I want to hate her, to take my jealousy and bash it over her head like a guitar, Pete Townshend style, because it is so big and violent, but I can't. I am too busy being proud of my slightly rotten little sister. She blows the boys away.

Yes, even Ty.

A faint rush of cold air swirls around my ankles as I lean down into the fridge, trying to find a place to wedge the ketchup bottle. The sticky red ring that it normally lives in has been swallowed up by a shifting load of jars and jellies, all jammed in.

"I think I should have just one name," I hear Billie say.

I stand up and rest my arm along the top of the open door.

My dad glances over his shoulder and then turns back to the sink.

Billie has pink streaks in her hair and fake tattoos stretched up her arms. She is wearing a wifebeater and booty shorts with her worn-out black leather boots.

She flexes her biceps. "Like Pink."

Dad turns off the tap.

"Or, you know," she says, dancing around and watching her reflection in the darkened windows above the kitchen table, "like Madonna did."

"Does," Dad says.

Billie stops dancing. "What?"

"Madonna's not dead," Dad says.

"Are you sure?" Billie asks. He nods, and she starts dancing again.

I finally give up and cram the ketchup bottle in next to Winston's homemade bitchin' hot barbecue sauce. (His secret? Lemon pepper.)

"But you're my Billie Carter," Dad says, sounding like his pride is wounded. Dish soap bubbles drip from the ends of his fingers.

"Yep," I say as I swing the fridge door shut, "named after the dishonorable brother of our thirty-ninth president. And a can of beer."

I memorized these facts in the third grade, back when I half expected to see my mom on *Antique Roadshow*, her hair done up, a can of Billy Beer in her hand, waiting in line to learn of her riches from a snobby guy with a bow tie and a Boston accent. But it was always just people with crap from basements and attics and the Civil War, nothing good.

She once brought home a can of Billy Beer from a garage sale—unopened and covered in dust—thinking it would be worth money someday. It sat on a shelf in our garage for years, and I thought she took it with her when she left. Turns out, Winston used it for target practice. Shot a hole in it with his first BB gun.

These days the beer story is just good ammunition against Billie.

She likes to pretend she is named after Billie Holiday, but it seems that we all were named after the shit my mom encountered during her daily trips to the convenience store or the flea market: cigarettes or beer cans or cheap nylon lingerie in a plastic bag. Go figure.

Billie pauses and gives me the finger.

My dad sighs as she stalks out of the room, the loose sole of her boot flapping along behind her.

"What's going on with you two?" he asks.

"Me and beer can Billie?"

His brow furrows. He is acting like he has never seen Billie flip me off before.

I shrug and reach for the dishcloth to wipe the table.

"Consider yourself lucky, Teddy Lee," he says, leaning back so I can run the cloth under the tap in front of him, "you came close to being called Quinn."

I start wiping. "That doesn't sound so bad to me."

Marginally better than being named after a dollar store negligee.

He smiles wickedly. "Short for Harlequin."

I groan.

"Yeah," he says distractedly, bending over the sink, "Your mom was really into romance novels at the time." He turns to grin at me, and a plate slips between his fingers and lands with a sploosh in the sink.

I finish wiping, and he pulls the plug. While the water gurgles down the drain, he dries his hands.

"How come Billie doesn't have a middle name?" I ask.

I have always wanted to know but never asked before. I bet Winston probably knows.

My dad's eyes light up, and I hold my breath as he crosses his arms and leans against the edge of the sink. A moment like this, just the two of us talking about the past, is rare. He remembers so much and tells us nothing.

I wish for a happy story filled with smiles and sunshine, instead of the darkness that I know. Does it hurt him to remember? Does he wish for a different ending? I'm not sure if I want to know.

"I guess your mom just ran out of gas," he finally says with a shrug.

His eyes clear, and just like that—snap—he turns back into himself, a tired man with three kids, wrapped in flannel nine months out of the year.

"Make it right with your sister, Teddy Lee," he tells me, his shoulders moving in steady, small circles as he starts to dry the dishes. He hands me a glass and a plate to put away. "You know I count on you."

My plan is to sneak Billie out of school. I'm pretty sure that isn't what my dad had in mind when he told me to make it right with Billie; but I know her best, and nothing will make her happier than skipping out.

I wait for her outside the girls' locker room after her fourth-period gym class. She is wearing striped tights and a long T-shirt pretending to be a dress and bounces on her toes as soon as she sees me standing against the windows, swinging my car key around and around on my finger.

We walk down the hallway as fast as we can, trying to keep our boots quiet on the dark green tile, checking both directions for adults and slowing down for open doorways as we go.

I do my best not to contribute to Billie's delinquency, seriously I do, but if Dad had something else in mind last night, he should have been more specific.

"Best idea of the day," Billie says quietly as she ducks under my arm and we sneak out the doors closest to the gym.

We crouch and run across the student lot, jumping over the crumbling parking bumpers and crooked feelers of crabgrass growing up through the cracks in the blacktop.

"What are you missing?" I ask her while I pump the gas pedal in my car just to be sure all systems are go.

"Interpolation."

She rolls down her window as we drive along the circular drive in front of the school. Billie is like a dog: she is always up for going anywhere, and she always has to have the window rolled down.

"You?" she asks.

"American government."

I drive through town, considering that there might come a time when I will regret skipping out on the electoral college. But the sun is shining today. The air is cool and fresh; and Billie is humming along to some tune playing in her head and leaning out the window. Right now it does not seem likely.

We pull up into an angled parking spot at the drive-in. It has looked the same since we were kids: a dark brown hut with a bright orange stripe painted around the base of the square roof. The carhops wear old-time change belts and come right over to your car with your food when it is ready.

I reach out to press the button on the illustrated menu/ speaker so Billie can order.

She leans past me and sticks her head out my window.

"Let's see . . . ." She studies the menu with her tongue poking out, like we haven't been here millions of times before.

"We'll have two cheese nachos and two—" She turns to check with me on the soda size.

"Medium?" she asks me. I nod. I hate talking to the machine.

"And two medium root beers." She finishes ordering and drops back into her seat. The two old guys in the car next to us look disappointed her ass is no longer on display.

"Not diet!" she yells as I start to roll the window up, and I jump.

"You done?" I ask, stopping with the window halfway so there is room for the tray.

Billie nods. "You know I hate diet."

I do. Billie would live on pure sugar if she could.

It is cold today, so our carhop has on a dark brown windbreaker when she delivers our nachos and sodas.

"The ones in the summer are better looking," Billie says, eating a chip and staring blankly out her window as our carhop walks away.

The nachos are covered in that fake bright orange, practically government-funded kind of cheese. They ladle it out of a large black pot and pour it on top of round, salty corn chips here. I'm sure you could get better nachos almost anywhere else in town, but these totally do it for me.

We sit silently, munching on our chips and taking long, slow sips of root beer. Billie eats in small bites, the cheesiest chips first, then scraping as much cheese as possible onto the ones left over, until she runs out and comes scrambling for mine.

We used to come here a lot with my mom. She could make an order of fries last all night. Billie and I would climb over from the backseat, into the front, where life was far more exciting, full of buttons to push and broken bits of Wint O Green Life Savers stuck into the crack of the seat and an always overflowing ashtray.

The radio would play low as the carhops swung back and forth in their white sneakers and short shorts, me in the middle and little Billie kneeling at the window, watching the world go by.

When it got dark and it was time to go home, we'd slide back over into our seats. Mom would drop into reverse, and we'd bite into the whole Life Savers we'd secretly stolen from her purse, leaning in close to each other so we could see them spark in the dark.

Billie licks her finger and dips it in the drift of salt left behind by her chips. She leans down and runs her tongue along the edge of the plastic tray.

She sighs.

I wish we had a radio.

The ice is melting in my soda. I give it a swirl and stare out over the dash. Somewhere down the road and what feels like a lifetime away, a school bell is ringing for us.

"Look what I got," Billie says.

My head rolls toward her along the back of my seat. Should I tell her she has cheese in her hair?

She digs into her bag and holds up a pack of Life Savers, Wint O Green and brand new, dancing it toward me with a big smile on her face. I smile back. I made it right.

Her fingers peel back the foil wrapper, and she hands me one.

I pop it into my mouth. Lean in close and bite down.

"Did you see it?" I ask.

The cheese in her hair shakes, and she hands me another one.

We are two tiny little girls, sliding around in a big backseat with minty fresh breath, all the way home.

7

"Got your next gig," Winston announces as he steps into the garage the next Friday afternoon.

It is the end of April, and the sun has been shining for almost a week straight. That is a seriously long sunny streak for us in Oregon. A trail of dust follows him across the threshold, sparkling and swirling up into the sunshine that angles through the windows.

He has been wandering in and out all afternoon, his old flip phone cradled on his shoulder. That thing has more miles on it than my car. A lit cigarette dangles from his lips. He is hustling for something, I can tell.

Jay's amp hums, a tense undercurrent, as we all freeze, staring and surprised. Without saying a word, Ginger Baker walks over and gives it a sharp, small kick.

"Uh, don't you mean first gig?" I ask.

"Semantics." Winston dismisses me with a wave of his hand before he walks back out the open door and into the yard, his mission complete.

A flood of nerves smacks into the mountain of excitement building in my belly and leaves me overwhelmed. I glance around the garage. Is it possible we'd made Winston into an overachiever after a lifetime of just getting by?

"But we don't have a set yet," Jay says to the four of us, his voice rising.

"A set?" Billie gulps. "We don't even have a name."

"Sure we do." Ty answers from the back of the room. "It's Red Velvet Crush."

"Red Velvet Crush?" Billie twists around her mic stand to look at me.

"What does that even *mean*?" Jay asks, pulling the strap off his guitar. He sets it in the corner next to an old broom and then runs his hand across the top of his head, rubbing his short hair. I didn't think he'd be so inclined to panic.

"You know . . . ," Ty starts to explain, his eyes checking in with me as he starts to articulate something that I myself have never tried to define. I mostly like how the words sound all strung together. I focus in, curious to hear what it means to him. "Sweet. Rich. With the potential for serious damage."

I suck in my breath and hold tight to my guitar. That boy is perfect.

Billie sets a half-eaten Pop-Tart on top of the amp in front of her and dusts the crumbs from her fingers. "We are not rich," she explains, as if Ty were an idiot.

"Don't be so literal, Billie," Ty says.

He points one of his drumsticks at me. "Sweet."

I blush a little bit.

And Jay. "Rich."

Jay looks down and shuffles his feet, even though it is true—and literal.

Then he points at Billie. "Potential for serious damage."

I smile at Ty, pretty much delighted with his explanation, even if it does make Billie sound more interesting than me.

"Besides," he says to Jay and Billie, "you're forgetting. We have covers."

"Are we a cover band?" Jay asks, his eyes big, suddenly a soprano. "I thought that was just where we were starting."

Ginger Baker cringes so hard it is almost audible.

I am with them. I have no intention of always being a cover band, but I don't know what we are yet. We haven't even had a chance to talk about it.

I honestly didn't think we'd make it this far. We are only six weeks in to being a band. So far I've been looking to keep Winston employed, Randy on our good side, and Dad happy.

I figured we'd make it only a couple of days, a practice or two into the musical experience, before Winston would bail, ditching us for something better or shinier or faster. But he is still here and actually trying. So covers of classic rock are fine until we figure ourselves out. We are working on some newer stuff, too, some Interpol for Ty, Editors for Jay, and a little Shooter Jennings to round things out when Randy is ready for it.

I watch Winston through the garage window, pacing in a circle in our side yard, his mouth moving faster than his legs. His left arm swings up into the air, punctuating the speech he is giving or promise he is making. I wonder what else he is getting us into.

He has the same long legs, the same bullshit smile, the same loud laugh as always, but I'm not used to the go-getter my brother has become.

Until now Winston has given up on everything: high school; his career as a kick-ass martial artist, which lasted three karate lessons (he claims his boys never felt comfortable in a gi); the thrill of motocross; even Emily, the one girl who actually seemed to love him and stuck around for a while.

She was great. She had this soft curly hair and a round face. Her lips were red and bowed up at the corners, like the cupids you see dangling from the ceilings in elementary school classrooms on Valentine's Day. She was sweet and smart and, for some reason, truly smitten until Winston went and ruined it.

I heard them fighting late one night a few years ago as I shifted around in my bed, Billie's breathing a hushed rustle in the background. Even in anger Emily's voice was soft. It curled under my door and across the rug.

"Why did you do it, Winston?"

I couldn't hear his answer. His voice was too low and muffled.

"I hope she was worth it," Emily said clearly.

There was a pause, and then I heard the front door close quietly but firmly before her tires crunched down the driveway and her headlights crossed my ceiling as she drove away.

We never saw her again. I hoped Winston felt like shit.

Why would he do anything that would risk her? Make her leave? Didn't he realize who she was? What she was? There would never be another Emily. There were a lot of Tinas and Brittanys and, for some reason, Cheryls. Yuck.

Then, the summer after Emily left, some stereos and other AV equipment went missing from the high school. It was a big deal at the time, with local crime fighters knocking on our door, but Winston was away from home, suddenly, and fortuitously, attending broadcasting school.

Life without him was too quiet, too cold. The cable went out, and there was no one to fix it. I wrote a lot of songs about snow and ice, even though we never had much of either one here where it is always wet and green.

Eventually the PTA coughed up enough cash to replace the TV sets. Then old Mrs. Crawley and her bony ankles, along with the rest of the faculty, finally got to sit back down, dim the lights, and get back to some serious teaching.

They also bought bars for all the first-floor windows.

Though he has never copped to the crime, I have always wanted to ask Winston: Couldn't you have stolen something less useful, like the sewing machines or the uneven bars?

Winston dropped out of broadcasting school last spring, and since then every word out of his mouth has sounded like a damn commercial.

Outside the garage, he laughs loud and continues his phone call.

Ty lifts up off his stool and cuts to the chase, getting to the important detail that the rest of us have overlooked.

Cupping his hands around his mouth, he yells toward the yard, "When?"

Winston reappears in the middle of the doorway. He holds up his finger, listens for a second, then answers, "Randy says next Friday night."

His answer fills the garage with electricity. Next Friday night isn't that far away. I feel more combustible than those cans Winston has hidden in the corner, pumped full of anticipation.

Ty nods at Winston: message received.

Winston flicks his cigarette butt into the air and casually walks away. Like a tiny firework, it sparks and blooms before it crashes onto the well-worn concrete. I imagine a blue streak burning its way toward us, a vapor trail streaking along the floor, rushing forward from spark to flame to hit man, with only seven days till we all explode.

Tonight is the night. We are finally going on last at The Night Owl, an armpit of a bar out on the highway, where everyone knows Winston by name so it doesn't matter that we are all too young to be on the premises, let alone onstage.

The sound of rain dripping off the roof and the clank of Dad putting pot lids away fill the house. Billie and I are in our bedroom. Winston took off in my car hours ago, promising to come back in time to take us to the show. His rusty 280Z is parked in our front yard, hood open, gutted like a fish.

I lean over and turn on the radio next to my bed. I tune it to the country station we like to listen to on the weekends and then empty my makeup bag onto our dressing table.

Putting on makeup calms me. It takes the shakes out of my hands and gives me something to think about other than the changeups we have been practicing all week and what we will do if no one shows up at all tonight and we end up playing to an empty room, dead silence.

Plus, if I have enough eye shadow on, maybe nobody will know who I am onstage. It is like camouflage.

"Now do me," Billie says, her blue eyes round and big as she leans over my right shoulder and crowds me right out of the mirror.

Billie always likes it when I do her makeup. She sits on the stool in front of the dressing table, cross-legged and patient. The dressing table was another gift from Grandma. It is curved and painted Dutch blue, with a large oval mirror.

If it weren't for that old woman, we'd all be sitting on the floor in a bare room, huddled around an old milk crate and a black-and-white television set.

Billie angles her chin up. She knows how to stretch her eyes just right so I can get eyeliner along the lower lash. She is a pro.

We have been practicing since she was eleven and Dad decided that makeup was okay, for fun—at home.

She likes to find ideas in fashion magazines and tear them out so we can try them later. The wall around our dressing table is covered in magazine pages: lightning bolt nails, hot pink lips with matching eyes, batwing blue eyeliner and black mascara.

Billie reaches up, smooths her hair over one shoulder to keep it off her face, and quickly twists it into a braid.

"What about a loose braid like that?" I ask, nodding toward her reflection before I put shadow on her brow bones. It glitters in the lamplight. It will twinkle on stage.

I add two coats of mascara. She blinks, and I wipe.

"Don't you think I'd dance it out?" she asks, stretching her face toward me, her lips pouted.

"Maybe," I say, searching the top of the dressing table for

the honey-colored lip gloss I know she likes because she keeps trying to steal it from me.

She rocks her head left and right, just barely, and the braid slips out.

"Okay, probably," I say.

I put gloss on her lips with the smallest brush. Dropping the brush back into my bag, I look her over. My fingers sweep an eyelash from her cheek, and then I give her a nod.

She stands, eyes down, trying to keep her back to the mirror. Billie doesn't like to see herself until the look is complete, head to toe.

"Beat-up blue jeans?" she asks, stepping into our closet.

"Yeah." I sit back down in front of the mirror while she digs around in the back of our closet. I hear a *zzzipppp*, and then she is posing in front of our pile of dirty laundry, wearing the oldest pair of jeans known to man.

They are also the best jeans ever, patched and repaired and held together by pieces and parts and lots of love. Once they were Winston's, then they were mine, and now they will eternally belong to Billie.

Winston got too tall, I got too curvy, but Billie stays the same. A perfect fit. I am still getting over it.

Billie kneels down in front of the closet and starts sorting through our shoe collection. A soft drum is tocking from the radio, and I hear Dad's boots coming down the hall toward our room to say good-bye. His steps match the rhythm of the Lady Antebellum song that is playing.

He walks across the pink rug and scoops me up into a small two-step between our twin beds. With his hand on the small of my back, he leads me around the rug in my bare feet for one ambling turn about the room.

A boot bounces to the floor as Billie leans out of the closet to watch us.

"Break a leg tonight," Dad says as he returns me to the dressing table.

"It's not musical theater, Dad." Billie rolls her eyes, sitting in a tangle of boots and sneakers and stretched-out sandals.

Dad reaches down for her. He slides her up into his arms and twirls her on his finger like a ballerina. "Good luck then," he says.

He lets her go and crosses the room. One big hand grips the door frame as he looks back and says, "Be safe tonight. Wish I could be there."

"Me, too," I say as he retreats. But he has to work. Like always.

"Boots?" Billie asks, suddenly standing next to me on one leg.

She has on one black boot, the ones that lace up the front, and one red rain boot that has a frog face painted across the toe. Someone's been raiding the boot bin at Goodwill again.

She flamingoes, helping me to choose.

"Black," I say. No question.

She bends over to lace up her boots.

I turn and face the mirror, sliding my hands through my hair, smoothing out the tangles. Moving in toward the glass, I study myself. Something is missing. I reach for my favorite eyeliner and stretch my eyes wide.

"Blue?" Billie asks, sounding skeptical, coming out to watch me smear the dark blue liner into my lash line.

I nod, unapologetic. I like it.

Outside our window Dad is leaving for work. He makes his way across the front yard as wrapped up against the weather as a grown man allows himself to be. He throws a stick for the neighbor's dog, watches it run, and then climbs into his truck, gone.

I finish my makeup and turn around. Billie steps out into the middle of the room. She is ready: black boots, beat-up jeans, and shiny blond hair swinging loose and long over her right shoulder.

I stare, my mouth open and my heart sore.

Taped in the medicine cabinet, just above the rusty shelf, where Dad's razor sits surrounded by a sprinkling of whiskers, is the one and only picture we have of my mom. Billie looks exactly like that picture, secreted away and suspended in time, minus the peeling Scotch tape at the corners. She takes my breath away.

My mom didn't look like the other moms. She was hotter. And looser somehow, like she could be easily disassembled.

Something was always sliding off her shoulder or drifting unbeknownst behind her. The dads and older brothers always stared.

"Candy's here, lock up your husbands," the wives whispered through pursed lips as she moved along.

I hated it. It made me hold tight on to her hand and want to drag her away with my little pink fingers, back home where she was only ours.

She was fragile.

Dreamy.

Breakable.

I am darker. Rounder. Built. With my dad's eyes, dark hair, and full lips. Billie is so blond she could wash away without a second shampoo.

She cocks her hip, holding her hands out. The ta-da is silent.

"Beautiful," I say finally, because she is, and I scooch over so she can see for herself.

Winston honks the horn outside, and my heart skips. It starts up again, but faster than usual.

"Showtime," Billie whispers.

I look up at her in the mirror. She nods down at me.

I wrap my fingers around hers, and she holds on tight, pulling me up from the stool and out of our room.

We rush through the kitchen and run out into the wet night together, lights still on, door unlocked. We race each other across the front yard, toward whatever waits for us, ready or not.

"Nervous?" Ty slides me into the corner of the dark bar. My back is against the paneled wall, the edge of the stage a few feet away. He faces me, bumping his toes up against my boots.

"No." I lie.

Of course I am nervous. We are about to take the stage for our first show ever and follow a band that has been pretty damn good. They call themselves Propaganda and wear matching jumpsuits. The small crowd clapped for them. We aren't even color coordinated.

Ginger is wearing some kind of Frenchman's lab coat, buttoned up tight. It is peacock blue. Jay has on his specialty: the shrunken 7UP T-shirt that shows off an inch and a half of his belly every time he moves. It peeked out with every bend and lift as we hauled our gear out of his car and my backseat and crammed it onto this small stage.

Billie has on the black boots and the best jeans ever.

Ty is wearing a crown of laurels and holding the hammer of the gods. Kidding. He has on a dark gray T-shirt, jeans with drumsticks poking out of the back pocket, and his pink sweatband on his wrist.

I went with multiple tank tops, way too many bracelets, and the darkest, tightest jeans I have ever owned. I think they are made of a little bit denim, but mostly blue paint.

Ty grabs my fingers and pulls me up onto the stage. Billie takes her place next to me, and Jay and Ginger squeeze in behind us. Maybe one of us should've run out to get something red or crushed or velvet, I think as I look out over the smoky bar, because this is about to get real.

Our amps are plugged in. Our mics are lined up. Most of the overhead lights are pointing in our direction, except for one that is wonky and looks like it is headed for the parking lot.

The ceiling is low, not much higher than the one in our garage. I hope the acoustics will be better, though.

A series of high, rectangular windows—a lot like our garage door windows—face the parking lot. The pool tables are parked by the door, and the curved bar pokes out into the room. If people dance, it is between the tables or right up against the stage.

Most of the Propaganda fans cleared out as soon as they packed up, leaving The Night Owl almost deserted. I count fifteen people. We could have stayed home and called the neighbors over for a bigger show.

Still, my fingers are tingling and my stomach tightens. It is time.

Jay starts hopping.

Hop, hop, hop, just small little ones up and down on the stage, barely even noticeable, as he burns through that endless supply of energy he seems to have been born with. Billie joins in, the toes of her black boots scuffing forward with each little hop. Jay grins, and I join in, too. Hop, hop, hop . . . scuff.

Ty takes his seat, snaps at the sweatband around his wrist, and starts tapping a syncopated rhythm on the edge of his drum.

He adds in a little high hat: hop, hop, tchht . . . hop, hop, hop, tchht . . . hop, hop, tchht . . . hop, hop, hop, tchht. . . .

Ginger bounces his head along.

We are smiling and hopping and ready to go. The guys at the bar must think we are crazy.

Jay brings in a thrumming bass line, and we are off.

Billie jumps around, slamming and bumping into the amps, getting shouty and singing at the top of her range. She throws herself into it, tearing a new hole in the best jeans ever and sending the thick orange extension cords that we forgot to tape down slipping over the edge of the stage.

Jay tries to slam with her, but Billie bumps away from him, taking her place behind her microphone stand. I scoot out of the way, keeping up with the music, glad she doesn't want to mess around with Jay, but pretty sure she's bumped up against much stranger boys than him before.

Ty and Jay and Ginger are lightning fast. No transitions, they go from one song to the next, bouncing to the beat, barely giving me time to find my fingering or take a breath.

Jay's hopping and Ty's pounding get faster as Billie sings louder.

Our guitars start chasing one another. Jay's bass notes are out front, and my higher notes follow right along. Ginger joins in, too, like the rounds we used to sing in kindergarten: one voice started, then another, then another. Row, row, row your screaming electric boat, with guitars and stompboxes and a pounding bass line.

We make a couple of mistakes, but the crowd does not seem to mind. They nod along and whistle during guitar solos. Pitchers of beer bubble, and a girl in a hippie skirt gets up to dance, arms over her head, the song in her head moving much slower than what we are banging out onstage.

Jay keeps hopping: small, medium, bigger . . . huge. He doesn't stop until Ty pounds down the last beat and we are done. A single phone pops up at the end, glowing, and that is enough for me.

There is no backstage, no glamour. We finish, grin at one another while we are wrapped up in Jay's last quivering bass note, and then we jump off the stage to pockets of applause.

As soon as I land, Ty picks me up and hugs me tight, swinging me around in a big circle, the toes of my boots hovering above the dusty wooden floor.

I don't care that only fifteen people showed up. I don't care that my shoulder aches and my hair is glued to the back of my neck. This moment—it feels like everything. I close my eyes and swing.

When my feet touch back down, Jay jumps in close and

high-fives me. "Remember when I started hopping?" he asks. His eyes are bright, and I swear I can see his pulse beating in the side of his neck.

"I do."

"That was awesome," he says, clapping his hands onto Ty's shoulders as Billie bounces between Ty and me.

Winston heads over from the pool tables, poking his cigarette into the corner of his mouth so he can clap as he walks.

"Good job," he says, fist-bumping Jay and then Ginger's freckled fingers.

"Thanks, man." Ty bumps back.

I stamp my feet. They are still buzzing. I am surprised how much I could feel the music through the wooden stage. It vibrated ten hundred times more than our concrete garage.

Inside, my chest is buzzing, too. A swelling feeling of holy shit, we did it grows and grows until I am beaming. It has to be pride, but I'm not sure.

Anticipation and dread and excitement: I understand all those. But pride is new to me. I take a step back. I want to soak it in before the sweat starts to dry and I forget how this feels. I probably look like a smiling, sweaty idiot.

"Next time we should start bigger," Jay says, throwing his arms out, almost smacking Ginger as he moves in, closing up the circle.

A steady stream of smoke escapes from Winston as he

exhales and agrees. "Definitely." Then he turns toward the bar, zeroing in on the hottest waitress.

"Let's get this party started!" he says, heading for the other side of the room. Billie is right behind him, with extra-jumpy Jay and Ginger on her heels.

Before my boots can grip onto the dusty floor, Ty grabs my hand.

"Let's stay here," he says, pulling me back toward the stage.

"Do you mean forever and ever?" I ask, hitching myself up onto the edge of the stage.

"Well," he says, climbing up and scooting in close, "at least until we get paid."

Winston is at the bar, a fresh pitcher of beer pulled by the hot waitress in front of him, waiting for the bartender to cash out. The overhead lights dim. It is almost closing time. Last call.

Billie and Jay and Ginger are in a shadowy corner in front of the jukebox. Jay is unrolling dollar bills from his front pocket, and "Freebird" fills up the spaces between the clinking of glasses and the soft slam of the cash register drawer.

Tiny white Christmas lights twinkle from the rail above the bar.

"You don't want to join the party?" I ask.

"I'm good right here."

I lean in and rest my head on his shoulder.

It may seem like a small move, but to me it is huge. It is needy and dependent and feminine and says it all: I need you and I want you and I am trusting you.

Ty doesn't shrug me off. He doesn't even hesitate. He wraps his arm around my waist and pulls me in, warmer and closer.

Under my cheek is a small, secret bump where the bones of his chest are supposed to lie flat. I run my fingers over it carefully.

"Bicycle crash," he says. "While high."

I look up at him. He breathes in, his eyes distant, and it reminds me of Dad. There will be nothing for the longest time, and then there it is, spilling out, and you'd better be holding on because it is going to be fast and true and probably never mentioned again. I can't help it, my heart hammers.

"Who gets stoned and rides a bicycle?" I ask. Winston just sits. Or watches TV.

"My license was taken away for a while, so I had to ride my dad's Schwinn everywhere."

From the outside, he looks like a regular boy. A hot one, but regular, not wrecked or wrung out. I know better than that, though. It's not like you get a free tattoo the first time you roll a joint or check out of rehab.

I trace his collarbone and picture him airborne, waiting for the landing.

"The doctor in the ER didn't set it straight; maybe he

figured I deserved it. He wouldn't write me a prescription for pain pills either. My parents sent me to Shorehaven the next day all slinged up. The ER doctor was on staff there."

He laughs low in his throat. "He clapped his hand onto my shoulder every time he saw me. Swear to God."

Shorehaven is a private hospital outside town, hidden down a long curving driveway behind a wrought-iron gate. Cheerleaders from school disappear there every so often, usually the ones from the top of the pyramid, the cutters and anorexics and obsessive counters. What the hell did Ty do?

"No strong stuff at first," he tells me, reading my mind. "You know, occasionally some pot, but that seemed kind of dirty. Then oxy back when you could crush it, Codeine, booze, Percocet . . . Whatever I could get my hands on in the end."

He glances down at me. I don't know if he expects me to be angry or disgusted or totally freaked out. I am not any of those things. I am kind of amazed that he is telling me: flat out, up front, admitting to something that most people would try to push under the rug or pretend never happened until some unforeseen situation forces it out into the light later on and by then it seems even bigger and uglier because of the wait. The truth always finds its way out.

I remember the wasted nights and fights in the dark and Mom and Dad's voices chasing down the hall. Never knowing for sure what was going on, never hearing the whole truth.

I grew up in a house full of tangled bed sheets, dark circles under tired eyes, light sleepers.

Ty's fingers play along his leg. His feet wiggle to the music. His eyes search mine, asking if I will stay past the scary part.

I reach down and take his hand in mine, finally understanding why he sets himself apart, why his attitude and appearance are so straightedge. He is a little bit broken. But so am I.

I put my head back down onto his shoulder.

He had laid it all out for me. He didn't run.

"Are you done?" I ask.

"Yep."

He squeezes my hand. We sit by ourselves, leaning into each other, listening to the jukebox and the conversation humming from the bar until the twinkling lights go dark and it's time to go home.

The sun is barely beginning to crack through the window over Billie's bed when my cell phone rings the next morning. I scramble to slip it out from under my pillow. Ty's number glows before my eyes.

Why doesn't he just text?

I press the phone tight against my ear. "Hi."

"Hi," he says.

I roll over and switch sides, smiling at the sound of his voice and hoping we won't wake Billie.

Her pillow bounces off the wall over my head and knocks over our lamp.

"What was that?" Ty asks.

"Well . . . Billie's awake."

I slide out of bed. My toes curl when they touch the cold

floor in the hallway. I can't take any more chances talking with Billie in the room—we don't have another lamp.

The house is quiet; the sky, chalk blue.

"What are you doing later?" Ty asks. He sounds like he's been awake for hours.

I climb onto our couch and reach for the plaid wool blanket that is always hanging off the back. I drape it over my shoulders and tuck it in under my feet.

"Something good, I hope."

We canceled our plans to practice today . . . since we crushed our first gig last night and all.

Ty pauses. I can hear a car humming in the background, the rub of the tires on the road.

"I'll come pick you up," he says.

"Like a date?"

"Can you define 'date'?"

"Most people hold hands and eat pizza and watch movies. Or mini golf."

"Are we most people?"

I look around the room at the worn-out recliner, the Jack Daniel's ashtray on the coffee table, and the latest issue of *Motocross Magazine* that Winston left behind. "Probably not."

"What about The Wall of Sound?" Ty asks. "Was that a date?"

My toes rub together under the blanket. "I thought that was an audition."

Ty laughs. "What makes it a date then?"

I give it some thought. "Kissing."

"By that definition, does my basement count?"

Does it ever.

"Let's listen to some records later," Ty says.

I let my head drop back against the couch. "Can you define 'later'?"

"After this meeting I have to go to, but way before it gets dark."

The sound of the road in the background slows and drops away. I hear the soft bing, bing, bing as his car door opens before he pulls the keys. "I promise," he says, "there will be kissing."

I picture his bright smile in a foggy parking lot somewhere. His car door slams shut.

"Then it's a date," I say, and hang up.

I curl into the corner of the couch and set my phone on the cushion next to me. The kitchen floor creaks. I hear the poof of the gas burner, the click of the coffeepot. My dad peeks around the corner, looking embarrassed. Oh, God, he must have been there the whole time. He heard everything.

"I never see you up this early," he says.

"I never see you up this early," I say, pulling the blanket around my shoulders and slumping toward the kitchen.

He's usually up and out well before we wake up for school. He leaves money on the counter for lunches, sometimes a Post-it that says, "Buy milk."

I sit at the table and watch him making his sandwiches. Cheese. Meat. Cheese. Meat. Long pull of plastic wrap. The teakettle starts to steam. He reaches over and turns the burner off before it can whistle.

"How's it going?" he asks, dumping a packet of hot chocolate into a mug and setting it in front of me. Then he pours in the hot water from the kettle, and the dusty chocolate floats and swirls. He leaves enough room at the top for stirring.

"Okay," I say.

He hands me a spoon, waiting to see if there is more.

"Who was that?" he asks.

"Ty."

He looks at me, wary. I've never had a boy call me at the crack of dawn before.

He's heard us practicing, seen us hanging together in the garage. But up until this morning I don't think he knew about Ty and me. Now he wants to see the whole picture. He wants to know if we are serious.

Steam curls up from my mug. I should probably spill and tell him everything, but keeping Ty to myself is sweeter than any mug of hot chocolate will ever be.

I take the spoon, staying silent.

"Stir that," Dad finally says, nodding toward my mug.

Then he bends down and kisses me on top of my head before he walks away.

✷ ✷ ✷

I sit on my bed that afternoon, guitar in my lap and notebook by my side. I have the room to myself since Billie found a ten in the pocket of an old coat while digging around in the front closet and convinced Winston to take her to the mall.

The clock ticks. It is shaped like a cat's head, and its eyes flick back and forth on the table by Billie's bed, clicking away the thousands of impatient seconds between Ty's early phone call and when he is going to pick me up for our date.

I strum and then scribble, lost in the flood of songs rushing through my mind. I make a quick note about starlight on the top of the page and another about magic.

"The door was open," Ty says.

He's standing in the middle of my doorway in a halo of dust and sunshine. "It always is," I say as the notes drop away and I return to the real world. "We don't have anything to steal."

Ty quirks his mouth and pauses. The word 'true' is probably crossing his mind, but he doesn't say it.

"What were you playing?" he asks, moving in and grounding me.

"When?"

"Just now." He laughs, nodding at the guitar sliding off my leg.

"Oh."

My hand is frozen over my guitar, a twang of metal still skating along my skin. I've always been waiting for someone to ask what I am working on, for someone to want to know.

Winston and Billie and Dad hear bits and pieces as I hum and write, but it is background noise to them, filler, like the creak and hiss of the radiator. They never ask to hear more or for me to play that one again. I shift around on my bed, trying to cover the page with the body of my guitar, wishing my notebook were invisible.

"It's nothing."

"Come on . . . ."

He smiles, crossing his arms. His T-shirt stretches tight over the tops of his shoulders.

"It sounded like you were searching," he says.

Exactly, I realize. *I was. But now you're here.*

Ty reaches out and touches the half-hidden notebook page. The last word —'spun'—dragged off the margin when I looked up at him.

"I've been there, too," he says.

But he doesn't press. He stays silent. Waiting. For however long it takes, he holds on while I decide if I can let him in.

Everything I want to say to you is here, I think; *everything unsaid but felt, unedited and private and personal and rhyming is here, practically at his fingertips.*

All I have ever wanted or picked at or even attempted is laid out on these pages. And even though I am dying to let you read it, to let your fingers slide down and across what I have written, it will be like handing over my heart.

It is one thing to be seen, something else entirely to be known.

I can't meet his eyes, but I hand him the notebook. Because he's already told me his story. He trusted me first.

His hand, warm and steady, brushes mine when he takes it from me.

He doesn't say anything right away or for a while. He sits on the edge of Billie's bed, legs splayed out, reading with his eyes locked on the page, lips moving. Utter concentration. For a smart boy, he is a slow reader.

Please, I pray as he flips back and starts again at the beginning, just please know that my heart is in your hands, and it is small and fragile and not sewn together very well.

Yet here I am, offering it up like a fool to the very first person who asks.

The comforter wrinkles under his legs as he pushes back, getting more comfortable, carefully turning each page. He is way too big for Billie's twin bed. His back mashes against the yellow flowers we painted on the headboard when she was eight. He pushes her pillows to the side. He takes up all the space.

I lean forward, listening to his breath, to the skim of his finger on the page.

Finally he closes the notebook and looks over at me. His fingers tap along his thigh, his eyes flick over my face, working from my mouth to my eyes, then back again. The wrong look or word or reaction will rip me open, and thankfully, he seems to know it.

A smile dawns slowly on his face. His amber eyes see right through me.

"You've been writing a song about a boy," he says.

I am nervous and excited all the way to Ty's house. It's weird going on a date. We both know what we are going to do—probably at the end—but we don't talk about it, even though we want to do it.

We are going to make out. Touch tongues. Feel skin on skin and get a little bit sweaty as we breathe heavy, whispering secrets into warm ears and wrinkling up cotton shirts, condom wrappers, and couch cushions as we go. It's possible one of us might get bitten.

I slam the car door way too hard when I get out of the minivan. I slip on the grass in Ty's front yard. He grabs my hand and steadies me. I look up at a sky full of stars and know that no matter what we do tonight, sharing my songs was barer and truer than any friction of skin will ever be.

Still, I can't wait to taste him.

We hurry up the slope and push through the front door.

His house is quiet again. We drop our shoes on the rug and slip down the stairs without a sound.

"Where should we start this time?" Ty asks, standing in front of the bookshelf full of records. He is almost talking to himself, running his fingers across the tops of the album covers one after another. He reaches over and flicks a switch. The front of the stereo lights up, electric and blue.

"How about with: Where are your parents?" I ask.

Ty glances at me over his shoulder. "Where they always are, working." He holds out an album like a pointer and turns to face the room. "How else could we afford all this stuff?"

Sinking down to the floor, I study the soft leather sofa and chairs; the matching seashells, large and small; the framed photos and state-of-the-art electronics gleaming in the warm light. They all go together, like a picture from an interior design magazine.

Most of our stuff comes from dead relatives or Winston's suspicious trips downtown, or we find it curbside under a sign that says FREE! TAKE ME. Ask any poor person—eclectic is overrated.

I lay back and run my fingers along the carpet. It is bouncy and soft.

I want to escape into Ty's world of tree-lined streets and tall houses made from two-by-fours, squared and true and painted in the dark green shades of deep summer, where the furniture comes in sets and the power never goes out because somebody forgot to pay the bill.

The record player clicks quietly as an album drops onto the spinning platter below. Ty lies down next to me. The music is atmospheric, hypnotic.

He reaches for my hand, listening, waiting.

I wait, too.

One song. Two songs.

Finally I say, "I kissed you first last time, remember."

"I remember," he says, rolling toward me. "You skipped ahead."

Propped up on one elbow, Ty reaches down and traces a line across my stomach with his finger.

He leans down, close enough to smell and touch and feel.

"First things first," he says as he slides one hand under the hair at the back of my neck and kisses me. We roll across the rug until we end up with my back pressing against the soft carpet.

His hair comes to a small shaved point on his forehead that I trace with my fingertips. He closes his eyes.

His mouth slides down my neck in a rush; his lips are soft and warm.

Kissing him takes away the whirl that is Winston and the sink full of dirty dishes that is never not there, waiting for me. It all disappears, swirling down the drain with the dried noodles and bits of soggy bread.

It doesn't smell like smoke or grease here.

The TV isn't forever on, filling up the background with noise. Books are lined up, spines out, actually having been read at least once. There is always milk in the fridge.

I grab his shoulders. They are solid and strong, a perfect

place for getting lost, for letting go and making a choice that is finally just for me.

We knit ourselves together, tight and warm, closer and closer, until my body and my breath move along with his and my thoughts of home and everything else in this world slip into the background, like overflow.

His weight shifts. I feel the cool slip of clothing, a shirt, some jeans. I push my underwear down around my ankles, then over the tips of my toes.

Ty slides his head past mine, short breaths over my shoulder. And when it hurts, when a sharp pain stabs in a place I never thought possible because it is so deep and private, he slows, and I arch my back, pulling him to me until he surrounds me and swallows me whole.

When he shudders and stops, I kiss him. He tastes sweet, like always, with honey warm breath and just the tiniest bit of tongue.

boy, you are my star

There must be a secret romance conspiracy just for boys. A special class they take that teaches them how to lure us in. The forehead kiss, the warm, spicy smell, the lift of the right eyebrow. We are all defenseless.

How else can I explain why I am standing on Ty's front porch, about to meet his parents for the first time?

"Come on," he says, smiling down at me from the top porch step.

He pulls me by my wrists, leading me inside. "It'll be all right."

His mom and dad look at me with skeptical eyes. Their recovering son has brought home a girl who has no curfew, no rules, and no boundaries. She is the sister of a supposed pot smoker and serious libertine. She doesn't even own a dress coat. They might as well just throw him off a cliff.

Tenuous threads of trust stretch across the room, trying to support him, but they bend under the weight of my family history. They've heard of Winston. Somebody always knows somebody that knows Winston. His reputation precedes him.

He is an urban legend. More bark than bite. Somehow Winston makes everything he does seem more exciting and dangerous and illicit than it is, and the stories get out of control. Believe me, I've seen him do nothing more for weeks on end than sit and watch World War II raging on in sepia tone.

Why do boys love watching history on TV so much? It confounds me. Unfortunately Winston is too fast to fight for the remote. He's had years of practice. He can hold Billie or me away from him with a straight arm, no effort or strain showing on his face, as he flicks the channel or turns up the rat-tat-tat of a panzer attack. I can't bitch too much, though, since he did steal cable for us for Christmas a couple of years ago.

Ty's dad shakes my hand. He is a full-time linguistics professor and part-time pyrotechnic.

Winston will love that. One Fourth of July he blew out our streetlight with the biggest Roman candle I have ever seen. It took the city two years to show up and replace that streetlight, but Winston will have a big scar on his thumb forever.

Ty's dad has all his fingers. I checked.

He gives me the once-over. His eyes crinkle in the corners just like Ty's, and his dark hair is shaved short, too. When he looks away, I squint and hold my thumb up over the patch of hair on his forehead, trying to see what Ty will look like thirty years down the road.

I drop my hand when I realize Ty's mom is watching me. She is a pediatrician with brownish hair. Skinny on top, big on the bottom. I don't know. She looks smart.

"We hear that you and Ty are in a band together," she says as she pulls the handle on the refrigerator door. The fridge matches the cabinets, and the cabinets match her hair. I can hardly tell she is there at all.

I nod, and she goes on, gesturing toward all the art on the walls, the assorted musical instruments shining from every corner of the airy, open rooms. "We believe in self-expression."

As if that explains it all. Them. Ty. Me. Here in their kitchen.

A lazy spring breeze blows in through their open windows, fluttering the curtain above the sink. The house is so perfect and the three of them so polite it almost makes me forget that Ty has a problem.

His mom makes mashed potatoes and sugar snap peas and roasted chicken for dinner. I didn't know you could do that at home; we only ever get roast chicken from the grocery store for special occasions, already roasted, with the little legs tied together, sweating inside a plastic case.

Ty's mom's chicken has rosemary and lemons stuffed up

its butt. It tastes nothing like the ones from WinCo. It tastes like something Martha or Nigella would make.

Winston has it bad for Nigella. He likes to lie on the sofa on Saturday mornings, all hung over, and watch her bajongas bounce about while she cooks, dreaming of her tea and crumpets.

But thanks to Winston and my local PBS affiliate, at least I know what rosemary is. Otherwise I might think this chicken is choking with weeds.

The dining room is a Norman Rockwell painting. The dishes shine. Candlelight bounces and glows. Classical music drifts in from the other room. The table is set with a tablecloth and a runner. Chargers and dinner plates, scrolled with leaves and gilded boughs. Real napkins wait next to each plate, not just stacked up in the middle of the table or wedged into one of those plastic holder things.

I take the seat next to Ty's at the table, wondering if it was always like this, even before Ty started using, or had they come together in group therapy and this was the result? They all are so careful. The air is full of trying.

When my mom was trying, the house would smell like browning ground beef and cigarette smoke.

Of course, since she was my mom, she went overboard playing happy housewife and wore a ruffled blouse and matching pantsuit with her spatula. All the other moms had ponytails and wore yoga pants and ordered Domino's.

Ty's mom passes the potatoes. It is strange to have so much food in front of me and not have to fight Winston for it.

His dad reaches for the loaf of fresh bread resting inside a basket in the middle of the table. He butters two slices and tears through the first one, leaving the crusts behind on his bread plate.

Billie would bite your fingers off for that, I think as he adds the crusts from the second piece of bread to the pile on his little plate. We don't have a lot of dinner guests.

I remember to put my napkin in my lap. I leave the lemon slice in my water glass, even though it floats against my lips every time I take a drink and I want to fish it out. I smile and chew with my mouth shut and pass the salt as silently as the rest of them.

Ty's mom blinks at her husband over the middle of the table. "When you saw at your chicken that way," she says, breathing loudly and interrupting the soft sounds of silverware and Chopin that fill the room, "it makes me feel unappreciated."

She slices into the breast on her plate, her slim hands holding her knife and fork like surgical instruments.

I glance around, my eyes skirting the edge of the fancy white cloth. Ty's dad is chowing down, his knife pointing skyward, gripped in his right hand, his chicken sawn in half: guilty. He stops, composes himself, and continues to eat.

Tense and uncomfortable, I kick my legs under the table.

Ty never even looks up. I am more than glad to push back from the table and drop my napkin onto my plate when dinner is done.

"We've got this." Ty's mom stands and says. His dad starts stacking the dishes and blows out the candles.

Ty reaches for my hand. I think we'll head for the basement, but we cross through the darkened living room instead. A shaft of moonlight streaks into the room, shining across the top of the piano and lighting up a thick orange stripe in the middle of a Persian rug. Ty turns left at the hall, and I follow.

Up the stairs this time, toward his room.

He opens the door and switches on the light. A glowing globe lights up on the far side of the room, slowly spinning, blue and green and oceans and continents.

His room isn't that big. But it is crammed full of books and posters. Books line a wooden shelf behind his bed and are stacked up on the desk next to the window. Some are schoolbooks. I recognize those shiny white covers and spines, but most are fiction. Ty reads for fun.

I run my finger along a tall tower of spines, hoping none of them are science fiction. Another stack, just as tall, sits on the windowsill. I glance at the titles. When does he have time to read?

An acoustic guitar leans against the side of his dresser.

I avoid the bed, even though all I want to do is roll around on it with him. It has a dark blue comforter and plaid flannel sheets. We could wrinkle them up good, if only his parents weren't right downstairs, doing the dishes and discussing their feelings.

I check out his posters instead—Rage Against, Joy Division, Bowie, the old Bowie with the chiseled cheeks and the makeup—then the top of his dresser. He has three black leather watches and a bracelet with silver spikes.

"I went through a postpunk phase," he says. "I don't remember a lot of it."

He slides the bracelet out of my hands and puts it back on top of his dresser.

"And how long will you be paying for that—for the not remembering?" I ask.

"What do you mean?"

"Your parents." I lift my chin toward the door. "They can act real. I think I can handle it."

Believe me, I am used to a lot more burping and farting (Winston) and arguing and crying (Billie), on a daily basis.

He takes a deep breath in. "No, they can't."

"Why not?"

He exhales.

"'Cause then they would have to admit that they have problems and that they have a son who is a druggie and that no matter what they do they can't change that."

He turns toward me and shrugs.

"They can't undo it," he adds.

I guess the high expectations and the matching sheet sets and the dreams and wishes of doting parents could be a lot to live with. I don't know for sure. My mom left us in elementary school, and abandonment sets the bar pretty low.

I study Ty's face.

What was I thinking? That because he has a mom and a dad and soft skin that smells like soap, he would be good? Protected? That these things would make him impervious? He had found the most painful way possible to undo a lifetime of planning and promise and expectation.

"Is that why you did it?" I ask.

I step toward him, and he hooks his fingers into my belt loops.

His plaid sleeves slip down and cover his wrists. His eyes drop, too, darker and sadder and more serious than I've seen them before.

When he looks back up, I slide in close. His eyes meet mine, and he says nothing. He doesn't have to. I get it. Sometimes smashing the guitar to bits is more important than the song.

Ty rests two fingers along the back of my chair. We are backstage in the corner of a dank, dark room at Burches Bar, wiping the sweat off, sitting on old folding chairs and a maroon vinyl bench with a tear in it. Worn duct tape holds the stuffing in.

Ginger Baker sits on top of a cardboard box. He is so skinny it doesn't dent or buckle beneath him.

Our bodies steam in this cool, muted space. Broken barstools and cases of industrial paper toweling build a fortress on three sides of us. A janitor's sink with a dripping faucet banks us in on the other. The water drips at a steady pace, shining at me, but I can't hear it over the thump of the headlining band.

The room is still, except for the thumping.

I am wiped out. My hands are raw; my right shoulder is tight; my feet and legs ache. Is all that pain worth it? Hell, yes. I can think of few things better, and all of those can break my heart. Music never does.

Billie is picking at her fingernails. A drip of blood dries along the inside of her middle finger as her gold glitter polish flakes away.

She is only a few feet away from me, but Billie and I have never been this far apart before. The normally tight space between the two of us has become strained because of Ty. Part of me wants to fix that, to pull her close and go back to normal. Part of me is fine with her pulling her fingernails off.

"Do you want me to whip out my hurdy-gurdy?" Jay asks quietly, an odd question that sits, almost like a whisper, filling the dim air.

"I didn't think you had one," I fire back. We are way too American, and a few members short, for any attempts at a dirty Arcade Fire joke.

"Ha!" Ty's laugh is a quick, loud burst that splits through the muffled room.

Billie glances over at me unsure.

"Is it big?" she asks in a low, serious voice, and Ty and Jay and Ginger start cracking up like crazy. Ginger Baker laughs so hard his skinny shoulders shake.

Ty wipes tears from the corners of his eyes, and I sit back, admiring the strange little world we have created.

Here we are, all five of us together, gigging around town, quickly figuring out how to be a band, and occasionally finding ourselves telling bad jokes while trapped in a bunker built from paper towels. What are the chances?

I don't dare ask. I don't want it any other way.

Because we are finally getting good. Good enough that Ginger doesn't wince anymore when Billie strays, changing up phrasing or adding a run.

Good enough that Billie and Jay don't accidentally run into each other when they both decide to go insane at the same time, dancing and jumping and running like wild dogs penned in by the edges of the stage or the walls of our garage.

So good that the days without the three of them feel sad and long. Quiet.

All this past spring, they've worn out the path from the edge of our gravel driveway to the side door of our garage, the grass flattening and falling out from their trips back and forth unloading gear and showing up for practice.

They bring donuts on Saturday mornings, cinnamon and sugar and the worst one ever, maple. Every Saturday. Winston loves it.

They wave to my dad.

They honk at the end of our street before disappearing around that last corner in a blur of taillights; one quick little blast that says good-bye as they drive away.

They feel like family.

A shaft of light falls on each one of them in turn—the tall one, the fast one, and the perfect one as Winston pushes open the door marked NOT AN EXIT and walks in. He has a wad of singles in one hand and a gleam in his eye.

I try to duck, but he ruffles my hair with his hand as he crosses behind me, as if I were a kid or a dog. His fingers leave a cool streak on my sweat-soaked scalp.

He stops at the bottom of the steps that lead back up toward the stage. "How would you like to go on the road?" he says nonchalantly.

There is a moment of complete silence. Then all the air is sucked out of the room in a whoosh. Am I the only one that feels it? I turn and look at Ty and then at Jay and Ginger. Their mouths are open, just like mine.

Billie starts bouncing up and down in her chair. Her half-glittered fingertips are pressed against her mouth, holding in a squeal.

Winston keeps on talking.

"Nothing big, just a few small clubs, you know, but still—"

"Like a tour?" I ask, dazed.

Who is this guy? I am used to the Winston who wanders around the house constantly looking for his lighter or stands in the kitchen shaking empty cereal boxes before putting them back into the cabinet. Not the taking care of business dude standing before me now.

Winston crosses his arms over his chest and smiles.

"Randy pulled some strings," he says.

It seems ironic that all I can feel at this moment is the pounding bass line of some other band.

"A freaking tour?" Jay hollers, his hands gripping the edge of the bench, arms flexing, ready to spring.

Winston nods. "There are still some details to work out, but if it makes you feel better, we'll call it a freaking tour." His grin is huge.

And Jay is up, jumping, his shaved head coming close to the low ceiling. He high-fives Ty, high-fives Ginger; working his way around in a circle. He high-fives Winston and then Billie, who shrieks and hops up high enough to hug him tight around the neck.

When Jay gets to me, I hold my hand up, dizzy and smiling. A dream I haven't even started to dream yet is rushing at me, with no chance to think or breathe or choose.

They all are so excited, but I want to sit. Maybe breathe

into a bag. Call for smelling salts. Something.

How did this happen?

Winston has never, ever done anything right before in his life, but he has somehow managed, pun intended, to be good at something, finally. And this is it, this is what he chooses: a road trip with his little sisters and a fledgling rock 'n' roll band.

My palm stings from the smack of Jay's hand. My fingers tingle and twitch. I let my hand drop.

Another hand, calm and warm and big, slides into mine, locking into my empty spaces and squeezing out the worry. Ty wraps me up, holding me tight and together while a roar of applause rises and fades a few walls away.

10

Winston sits at the table, a box of cereal and a bowl parked in front of him, spilled sugar surrounding his elbows. He lifts his chin toward me as I plop down and reach for the open box. I plan to sit right here until Dad comes home. I dig my hand into the box and eat the sugary flakes dry, calling them dinner.

Winston helps himself to another bowlful, shaking one, two, three more flakes on top of the mound. Then he grabs the milk and pours, slowing as the milk appears under the cereal, slowing again when the cereal starts to rise and float, skimming along the rim of the bowl: breakfast cereal perfection.

I have seen him do this hundreds of times. Winston is extremely proud of his ability to fill a bowl.

The back door swings open, and a couple of wet leaves swirl in along with Dad. He swipes his hand across his forehead and smooths his hair as he shuts the door behind him with his hip.

I play with some of the stray sugar that has escaped from Winston while Dad pulls out the chair across from me and sits down.

"Winston told me," he says, his eyes on the table.

I push the sugar aside, sweet and useless. I don't know what to say. It all happened so fast, and I wish I could have told him. Winston is too quick and harsh, his words coated in nicotine and braggadocio. I would have at least pretended to ask.

Billie spent last night with a packed duffel bag next to her bed, as if the tour could happen at any moment without notice. But I'm not so sure about it. Any lingering bubbles of excitement inside me burst as soon as I woke up this morning, smelled Dad's coffee, saw Billie's toes peeking out from the end of her blanket.

I'm not worried about the hard work, or the music, or the trip itself. I'm worried about Dad and me. This place is my home. He is my ballast.

He stayed. He held on with his warm, sturdy hands when Mom let go. I don't know if I can just walk away from that and leave him here, alone.

And I have only ever been here, known here. I wish I could be like Billie, so ready to go, but I don't know if my brain works anywhere else. What if my music doesn't follow me down the road, away from this place?

Dad stands, grabs the back of his chair, and pushes it in slowly, right against the edge of the table, carefully lining his thumbs up along the worn back. I sit up straight, grateful that Winston is too busy chewing to chime in.

"Let me think about it," he says, and my head hangs low, sinking toward the table.

I nod and press down on the stray sugar in front of me, feeling it crunch under my fingertips.

It winks in the late afternoon sun, daring me to taste it. It leaves only a fleeting sweetness on my tongue as Dad walks away and my brother pours himself another perfect bowl of breakfast cereal for dinner.

"Couldn't he just get a job at McDonald's?" Dad asks a week later.

We are putting the groceries away. Two paper bags stuffed full that Dad carried in from his truck, the tops wet from riding around in the open bed all morning. Somehow it always ends up just being the two of us on Saturday afternoon, when the job of unpacking comes around.

Today I am hanging at home on purpose. Not for the groceries but because tonight is Ty's graduation. I spent the morning inspecting my dress and picking out just the right pair of shoes and staring in the bathroom mirror, wishing that my teeth were whiter.

"Winston?" I ask, turning the cans of vegetables in the

cupboard so that the pictures of corn and beans and peas all face out. It looks like we are neat and organized and temporarily flush with cash. Before Winston messes them all up anyway.

"You know he won't," I say.

If that were an option, Winston would have done it years ago. But there's no way he'd wear a uniform or fit into a drive-through window.

And what happened to my dad's love of Winston's job at the radio station? He seems less enamored with it now that it means we might be going on the road.

He shakes his head, not really listening to me.

I'm not sure I even need to be here. I am merely a witness to the internal argument he has been having all week, the debate that must have been raging inside him since Winston broke the news. We might be leaving home. All three of us.

Following behind him, I pick up the things he leaves stacked on the counter and then straighten out the packages of sandwich meat and sliced cheese he stuffs into the fridge, all in the middle of the top shelf.

I spread everything out, even put a cucumber into the vegetable bin, so our bounty is evenly distributed. Will we ever find a reason to eat that lonely cucumber, or will I throw it out this same time next week, limp and wrinkly?

Dad stops in the middle of the kitchen with a can of coffee resting under one arm. The red lid glows as the afternoon sun banks in through the windows over the table, reminding us that spring is almost over.

"School will be out soon," he says, rubbing his whiskers with his free hand. It is his day off; whiskers are allowed. He sets the coffee on the counter, next to the pot. "And you'll be there to take care of your sister."

Neither seems like a question. So I simply stare back, letting him work it out for himself. He hands me a box of chocolate chip cookies, the big box with enough for everybody to get at least one after Winston has had his way with them and plenty of busted cookie dust at the bottom for Billie to stick her finger into.

I put it in the cabinet, far into the back corner, hiding it. Maybe I am hoping he won't let us go. That way we can stay home and everything will stay the same as always: safe and small and easy. But maybe I want more than that, too.

It is the perfect night for Ty's graduation. The air feels warm on my arms, and a breeze is blowing through the newly budded trees as I park my car.

Billie talked me into a sleeveless dress. I knew she would go out in a handkerchief if she thought it looked good, damn the weather, so I wasn't sure when she picked this one out at the mall. It fits snug around my waist, and the dark blue skirt flares around my legs like I am ready for a party.

Now I am glad she pushed for it because the cars I am

passing as I totter through the parking lot are all German, all expensive. All shiny and screaming, "We know you pulled up in a late-model Camry with a bad starter and a voracious appetite for synthetic motor oil."

Walden Academy is imposing. I need to be dressed up.

The building itself is old. The faded red bricks of the original structure have stood the test of time. Newer blocklike additions were built onto each side and cropped up from the back. I open one of the glass doors of the entrance, gripping the thick brass pull.

It is like stepping into a tent in a Harry Potter novel. The wooden floors and grand old tradition of the main entrance open up into a modern world of shining stainless stairways and bright glass-walled classrooms filled with world-class gadgetry.

The floors creak under my feet as I hurry across the lobby.

Just the divorced dads and I are arriving late, skimming in at the last second.

The catering staff is busy setting out crystal punch bowls and silver platters full of sugar cookies for after. Banks of mullioned windows flank me on my right, the glass slowly running for the floor, one century at a time.

I follow the hand-lettered signs set up on easels and make the turn toward the auditorium. A sea of black graduation gowns fills the hallway, waiting for the cue to enter. Ty and Jay are in there somewhere, inching toward their diplomas.

I hand my ticket to a large lady in a white blouse. The PTA sticker stuck to her chest says DEVON'S MOM.

"Thanks," I whisper, and slip through the open doorway.

The auditorium is an excited hush, a collection of whispers and quiet coughing and flash photography.

I smooth my skirt and slide into one of the few remaining aisle seats near the back. It has green velvet cushions and a little brass plaque engraved with a name on the curved wooden back.

My school has a gym for an auditorium, with metal bleachers that fold up against the walls. We have engravings on the seats, too, but they are scratched in. They say things like "Eat me." Or "Cheri is a coked-out slut."

The student orchestra is entering from the right, taking places along the risers set at the back of the stage. Thick curtains bank both edges of the stage, held sway by ropes, waiting for the next performance of *Pippin* or *Of Mice and Men*.

Ginger pokes up from the back row: a tall poppy in a sea of short brown grass. He positions himself behind the timpani, his eyes on the conductor. I smile. So Ginger Baker is a drummer after all.

With a quick flick and a sharp drop of the conductor's baton, "Pomp and Circumstance" fills the room. The kettledrums pound low and deep. Ginger's hair puffs to the side when the crash cymbals smash together next to him.

The doors at the front of the room open, and the graduates file in: a swishing procession of black robes. Almost all of them have gold cords strung over their shoulders. Applause buffets the curtains and bounces off the stage.

"Today is the day to set your dreams on fire," a tiny Asian girl says from the podium at the center of the stage when the noise dies down, craning her neck up to reach the microphone.

Isn't that a Taylor Swift song? My ears prick up. Sounds like it. Her parents must be so proud.

Are Ty's parents somewhere down front, saving a seat for me, the girl who is going to take him away from all this excellence? It is too late to check; dreams are ablaze all around me.

Parents are zooming in. Tablets and cell phones and old-school cameras crowd the horizon, arms reaching up for the best shot of this priceless moment.

"Pictures are for people who can't remember things," Dad told me—years before at Billie's eighth-grade graduation. He tapped his temple as the other parents fought for territory. "I remember everything."

It is true. He does remember everything. But maybe, just maybe, he didn't want a reminder of where we've been, a book full of photos to show the hole in our family. Either way, we have never owned a camera.

Winston bought a disposable cheapie for a school trip

to Disneyland once when he was in high school, but all we ended up with was a paper envelope stuffed full of two-for-one prints of girl's asses.

"Please hold your applause until all the graduates' names have been called," Ty's principal announces.

The graduating class lines up at the edge of the stage. Suddenly the aisles are swamped. Moms and dads block and tackle.

A woman in a tight black satin skirt kneels in the aisle next to me. A camera that probably cost more than my car presses against her face; her other hand grips my armrest for balance.

I don't stress, though. I don't even try to tip her over. (Just a little push, and that rock of a wedding ring would do the rest.) I don't need a picture to remember this night. I already feel legit, like a real girlfriend with a graduation program in my hand and a road trip on the horizon. Maybe I'll even write about it one day.

Jay is called before Ty. He crosses the stage, practically running by the time he reaches the principal. He pumps the principal's arm up and down twice, takes his diploma, and turns to pose for the cameras, still for only a second before he whoops loud and runs a fast lap around the edge of the stage. Everyone onstage waits patiently. They are obviously used to Jay by now.

Ty crosses the stage in two big steps—just like the first time I ever saw him—and the first few words of a new song fill my head. When they call his name, I don't care what anyone has to say. I clap so hard my hands hurt.

My phone buzzes late that night, after the sparkling cider and the cake and the congratulations. After I kick off the blue dress and climb into bed and write for hours. Until Billie, still in her coat, climbs into her bed across the room, and we both fall asleep.

"I'm outside," the text says, and I slip on a sweatshirt and wrap myself in my quilt and then walk on my toes all the way to the door.

It is clear and chilly. My nose tingles when I breathe in. The sky is dark blue, finished with black and already moving on to the colors of day.

Ty is standing in the far corner of the yard, staring at the house. The streetlight is out, again.

A mountain bike is dropped on the grass behind him, the handlebars stuck at an odd angle into the dirt. No minivan tonight; he is in stealth mode.

"I didn't know if your dad was home," he says.

"The answer to that is almost always no."

He holds his hand out, and I pull him toward the porch. We sit down on the top step, and I cover his shoulders with the quilt. His nose is red from the bike ride.

"I'm in," he says quietly in the dark. "They're letting me go on the road."

I can't see his eyes, but his voice sounds excited.

"That was their gift to me for graduation: my freedom."

It is probably more like trust than freedom. Trust—with a credit card attached for emergencies.

"Well, freedom, and some serious savings bonds." He laughs.

He reaches under the blanket and squeezes my leg.

"And Jay?" I ask.

"He's in. His parents are going to Europe for a couple of weeks anyway. He'd have to stay home with the housekeeper. He thinks she smells like mothballs," he whispers into my ear as if it were a state secret.

Jay seemed so excited before. Is he only going along to avoid the lady with a dustrag and a slight odor? Maybe *These Songs Are Better than Mothballs* should be the title of our first album.

"Life's rough," I say.

"No, not like that," Ty wiggles my leg. "You know Jay. He would've found a way, no matter what."

I picture Jay bouncing through a very clean house, smuggling a backpack stuffed full of T-shirts and sneakers of various colors past a geriatric housekeeper as he makes his escape. Yeah, that's better.

"Ginger?"

"Still deciding. It's the tour or a summer music program at Berklee. He thinks this"—he lifts one arm out from under the blanket and gestures toward the garage—"is better. His mom is heartbroken."

I never thought about Ginger having parents.

Created in a lab? Yes.

Spawned from robots? Possibly.

But a mom and a dad who got down and dirty to make him? Never crossed my mind.

God, what if everybody can go but Billie and me?

I take Ty's hand under the blanket and press my palm into his.

The sky is creeping up on us. I can see his eyes now, looking sleepy as he sits next to me, snug in the quilt that Winston used to sleep under when he was little, the one he got from Grandma Ruby, our mom's mom, the grandma that Billie and I never met.

It's got kittens on it, so Winston abandoned it once he started getting short and curlies. It was as if he were afraid those little embroidered kitties would wake in the middle of the night and chew off his tender parts.

The warning glow of the sun is along the horizon, still hidden by the trees that line the street. A new day is coming.

"I got you something," I say.

Ty shakes his head. "You didn't need to get me anything."

"Okay; then I made you something."

"Even better."

I slip a piece of paper out of the front pocket of my sweatshirt under the edge of the blanket. I can feel the twirls and loops of my words under my fingers. "Actually, I wrote you something."

"That's best of all."

It is a scroll, written and rolled on thick white paper, tied with a striped ribbon I stole from Billie's jewelry box.

I worked on it all night, ever since I left his party, slowly writing each word so there were no scribbles or misspelled words. I slide it into his hand.

Ty pulls the bow, unrolls the paper, and smooths it out along his leg.

As he reads, the last verse curls up at me from the bottom. I can hear the words in my head, the melody that goes along:

where did we start, and how does it end?

a note,

a whisper,

a promise made to keep,

and what do you see, twinkling before you when you sleep?

is it the stars,

the moon shining bright,

or is it me?

"Maybe I'll sing it for you someday," I say, my voice husky because he hasn't said anything.

He carefully rolls the paper and reties the ribbon with his big fingers. Just like new. He smiles out over the yard, then turns and squeezes me tight.

"Maybe I'll play it with you someday," he says.

He kisses me, once, and then we watch the sun rise from my front porch, a golden carpet spreading out before us, the song I wrote for him held fast in his hand.

"I guess I should get used to this," Dad says.

I am in the kitchen, staring at the blue flames hissing from the stove, waiting for the kettle to boil so I can make some hot chocolate, when he walks in from his late shift. I am still bundled up in my blanket, kitties turned inward, thinking of Ty pedaling away from me.

I turn to look at him. "To what?"

Steam, warm and wet, is beginning to rise from the kettle. I pull the quilt from my shoulders and start to fold it.

"To this," he says as he walks over to take the bottom edge of the blanket in his hands. "Silence."

We hold the blanket between us, the morning sun catching the quilted patterns, the shiny thread and soft worn spots.

He takes a step toward me, folding the blanket in half the long way. I smooth the edges.

"You staying up all night." He reaches down for the new bottom. "Boys riding away on bicycles."

"You saw Ty," I say as we fold the blanket in half again.

He nods, making the last fold. He pats the top of the quilt, which is resting in my arms. We are better than the Boy Scouts.

"His parents said he could go," I say.

"So that's why he was here."

He takes the quilt from me and, hanging it over the back of a chair, walks to the table, putting the countertop between us.

"I know what it's like to try to keep someone who wants to be gone, Teddy Lee," he says, staring down at the chair before he comes back toward me.

He looks like he did back when my mom would disappear for days, sometimes for weeks at a crack. She'd reappear with a suntan and a wistful smile, never with any explanations or souvenirs. We got a week or two of wearing the same underpants, and he got to struggle with the dishes and the Hamburger Helper. He looks lost.

I stammer. Dad holds his hands up, stopping me.

He reaches past me and turns off the kettle, catching it seconds before it whistles and wakes up Winston and Billie, still snoring down the hall. A steady stream of steam pours out of it, and I can hear the water dancing around inside.

I'm not sure what made him make up his mind. Maybe it was learning that the other parents had agreed and he thinks their children are far more breakable than his. His are already broken and glued back together. Maybe that makes it okay.

Or maybe he has finally found a way to live with it, another hollow ache that will throb less over time; a hole in his heart that he will remind himself to step over every day so he doesn't fall in.

He sets out my favorite mug, the white one with a rainbow across the front, and a spoon. Everything in the kitchen is only an arm's length away for him.

He straightens up, pours the water, and says softly, with his eyes on mine, "Just come back to me when you are done."

11

Winston and I are at our kitchen table the Saturday night after Ty's graduation, a map of the Pacific Northwest and the itinerary for the tour spread out before us.

Billie is sitting on the front porch, just outside the screen door with a cigarette that is at least 85 percent ash tucked between her fingers. She is trying to work some shorts, but it really isn't that warm yet. Smoke drifts in on the fresh start-of-summer air.

I watch her cigarette burning down to the filter as Winston double-checks Randy's notes and makes dots with a marker on each of the cities where we will stop. Portland, Bend, Eugene, Ashland, Yakima, Boise, even Pocatello, some spots in suburban Seattle, and almost every tiny town in between. Then a red star for home.

"No one is touching the Z," he says, overly concerned about his car. He stubs his cigarette out into the ashtray that is holding one corner of the map.

Transportation is the one minor detail that Randy and Winston have somehow overlooked during their intense planning. We are debating a caravan of my car and maybe Jay's.

How Winston forgot about transportation is beyond me. He lives for cars. And sex. And snack cakes. Yep, sex and cars and a creamy filling stuffed into straight-leg jeans: that's my brother.

I am practically clawing my eyes out, trying not to take over. Winston seems amazed that he has done something this well, and I don't want to wreck his moment; but his oversight isn't inspiring a lot of faith. I also don't want to walk when my car gives out somewhere near the base of the Three Sisters. It dies when I drive it through a deep puddle.

Winston has lists upon lists and a strange subcategorization system that involves checkmarks and asterisks and scribbles that look mysteriously like his pen is running out of ink.

It seems like he has everything figured out other than the car, but I can't be sure, I'm not wearing my secret decoder ring.

A beam of headlights crosses the yard, and Billie gets up. It is probably just Dad, home early. She swats at a bug that is circling her head; then she presses her nose flat against the screen door.

"You have got to see this," she says.

I push away from the table, glad to leave the marker smell

behind. Winston grabs his smokes and follows me out.

An old white van is pulling up into our front yard, leaving two strips of crushed grass behind it. I stop on the bottom porch step and stare.

It looks like Winston has been saved.

Jay is in the passenger seat with a baseball cap on backwards. He leans out the window, waving like a madman. CRAZY CARPET KING is painted on the dented sliding door. The words are faint, barely hidden by a thin layer of white paint that still has brushstrokes in it. A tiny silver crown topped with fake jewels dangles from the rearview mirror.

"Look what graduation got us," Jay says as the van lurches to a stop.

"Why does it sound like a lawn mower?" Billie asks.

Ty and Jay climb out. The engine is still ticking.

"Does it even have seats?" I ask, not dying to spend the summer riding around perched on top of a pile of rolled carpets.

"Better," Jay says, reaching over to pull the handle. He opens the sliding side door with a game show flourish. "A bench."

Covered in shag. Just like the walls and the floor and the ceiling, as if 1972 had puked all over inside, golden orange with brown flecks.

"Crazy carpeted it for free," Ty says.

"How lucky for us." I stick my head in and sniff. It makes me want to sneeze.

"Is it really ours?" Billie asks, stretching up onto her toes to see in over Winston's shoulder.

"Bought it this morning," Ty says, holding out the title.

It was signed over by Crazy himself.

Now I know where those savings bonds went. They are cashed out and parked at the edge of my yard.

I am kind of glad the van is ugly. That makes it feel like we are all equal. If we had to drive around all summer in a shiny new Sprinter, compliments of Ty and his generous relatives, it wouldn't be the same.

A new van would make me feel obligated, as if my hair always had to be washed and I couldn't wipe Dorito dust on the upholstery when necessary. And you need chips on the road . . chips and soda.

I lean back and cross my arms. Yep, this van is just ugly enough to work. Jay and Billie climb inside and shut the door.

School is done.

My dad said yes.

Winston has a plan.

The new old white van is ready and waiting.

"I guess Ginger's not going to Berklee," I say to Ty.

Inside the van Jay blinks the headlights on and off, and Billie blasts the horn.

"Guess not," he says.

"Good."

∗ ∗ ∗

Our room is a disaster. The closet door popped off the track. Socks and tights and tank tops spill out of the dresser, dripping over the edges of the open drawers. Shoes and boots dot the floor: total land mines when you aren't looking.

Billie is buried in a pile of hoodies and striped T-shirts on her bed.

We are supposed to be packing for the road. Billie has the bag she packed weeks ago stashed under her bed as a backup, so today she is mostly playing games on her phone and lolling around on top of the laundry I did earlier so we'd have half a chance at smelling fresh when we started out.

Propping a stack of sweaters under my chin, I navigate toward my bed.

"Shit!" I stop and rub my bare toes on my shin, caught by surprise by a high heel hidden under the edge of the rug.

I hate packing. With each fold, it feels like I might never come home again, and that makes me try to take everything I own with me, just in case.

We've never been far from home.

No relatives to visit, no summers at the shore.

God, we never even got to be Girl Scouts and spend the night in a musty tent. There was no such thing as sleepaway camp. The farthest away we've ever been are school trips to the Space Needle and slumber parties down the street.

Winston looks in on us on his way down the hall and shakes his big head.

"One bag," he says, "that you can carry."

The sweaters land on my bed in a heap. This new Winston is so bossy. I grab my duffel bag and start to chuck that mother full.

Dad's truck pulls up out front. The crunch of his tires carries in through the open window over Billie's bed and I look out at him. He's home early. Must have called in sick for his night shift.

"Let's barbecue," he says, meeting Winston halfway across the front yard. He is carrying a bag of groceries by the handles. Carrot tops, or something green, pokes out the top of the bag.

I raise my eyebrows at Billie. She pops up and peers out.

"Vegetables?" she asks, climbing out from the pile of clothing on her bed and walking with me toward the kitchen.

Winston sets his phone onto the counter and immediately starts mixing up his secret sauce.

Billie and I get out the plates and the cups and the big platter we never use while my dad starts the grill. The platter has a chip in the side, but we pretend it is okay. It is the biggest plate we have.

Ty shows up just in time to hear the sizzle of the very first steak. Dad has splurged. We never have steak.

"You hungry?" Dad asks.

"Always," Ty answers.

Dad grins and turns back toward the grill, poking and flipping. The sun is almost set, and sweet, meaty-smelling smoke drifts in the air. It is June and the peonies are blooming and it is our last night at home, our last dinner together before we leave.

We sit around the fire, talking and eating while the sky gets dark. We pass the steaks around on the big platter and then the sauce. The carrots went into a salad that Billie and I put together, even making the dressing ourselves.

Dad closes the lid on the grill and hangs the tongs from the handle on the side. He pulls his chair up next to mine and sits down in the summer darkness.

Winston prods the coals of the bonfire with a long stick over and over, never content to just let things burn. His feet are resting up against the rocks that circle the flames, the bottom of his shoes smoldering. They smell like they are starting to melt.

Sparks shoot up from the jabbed-at embers, glowing hot and bright and then gone into the night.

The front of me feels cooked.

Ty's head is back, resting against his chair, staring up at the starlit sky. Billie is curled up in a lawn chair on the far side of the flames, knees tucked into my sweatshirt, stretching it out. Her chin is down, her eyes glossed over, hypnotized by the fire's flicker and pop.

The food is long gone. Mismatched steak knives rest on the empty plates at our feet. Winston's sauce has worked its magic; there isn't a drop left.

"Get my guitar," Dad says, reaching over to pull on my sleeve.

I raise my eyebrows and look his way, lazy from the heat. He never plays for us. He only plays late at night when he thinks we are asleep, keeping his voice low and the music quiet.

He lifts his chin toward the house and urges me on.

"Come on," he says. "It's getting late."

I stand, balancing my plate on my arm, and reach down to take Ty's, too. He sits up straight, handing his plate to me with a curious look. As far as he knows, my dad stacks palettes and survives on tuna salad sandwiches, and that is it. He doesn't know there is music involved.

I blindly set the plates on the kitchen counter, reluctant to turn on the light inside and break the spell cast in the backyard by the fire and the food. I can hear the hum of the refrigerator, the soft thud of my shoes in the hall as I walk toward my room.

I know which guitar he wants. He has two in his bedroom, a black one and a blue one, but he wants the original, the one I borrowed from him so long ago with the stars and the moon on the strap. It is in my room, resting against my headboard, ready to go on the road.

My bed is made, only a dent left behind where my duffel bag has been. Now it is packed and waiting by the front door. Billie's bed is made, too, somewhere under the stuffed animals and mass of unfolded laundry.

The moon is shining in over her bed. Her music box sits

open in the middle of the rings and bracelets and wrappers on the top of the dresser. Our room is messier than it has ever been, even though it is about to be empty.

I feel homesick. I will miss this room, messy or not.

I smooth the dent from my blanket and unsnap my guitar case.

Pulling the guitar out, I glance around the room one last time. I reach over and tear a tiny piece from the wallpaper beside me and tuck it inside my case, a faded gold and blue corner that nobody will notice but me, a secret piece of home.

I head back toward the yard, Dad's guitar in my hand. My hip pushes the back door open. I catch it with my hand so it will close softly behind me.

Winston has a beer between his knees. A six-pack of glowing green bottles is planted underneath his chair.

They stoked the fire while I was gone. It is blazing.

I hand the guitar to my dad and sink down on the grass by Ty's feet, lower and closer to the warmth, wishing we had marshmallows.

Dad tunes the guitar carefully, adjusting the strap to his size.

Billie stirs.

Ty sits forward in his chair, and my dad starts to strum.

It is a shy, quiet start. It sounds kind of country but not sad. Then he sings, and his voice is this mellow smoothness, this highway that rolls and rolls and rolls, dissolving into an endless horizon. I want to stay here forever, where my dad's voice melts into the sky.

I lean into Ty's leg, looking up at him. His body sways, denim and muscles, as my dad plays. He taps along, and I can feel his vibration through the soft ground as he finds the structure beneath the song.

Winston opens another beer. *Hisss.* . . .

My dad changes keys.

Ty's eyes flicker. His face is flushed with firelight, his gaze growing bright with realization. He looks across the flames, considering Billie and then Winston, while Dad rolls one song into the next.

From star to star to star he moves—my sister, my brother, my dad, and then me—soaking us all in, connecting and understanding, finally seeing for himself how our constellation was built.

Somewhere in this world there are people with matching luggage sets. Large suitcases and small suitcases, the kinds that fit into overhead bins, with tiny, shiny combination locks and rolling wheels. We are not those people.

The back of the van is filled with backpacks and duffel bags and boxes wrapped in duct tape. I am pretty sure I see a plaid bowling bag in there, too, near the bottom.

My dad reaches for my duffel and throws it on top of the pile. Winston takes my guitar and slides it in sideways, as if it were the missing piece of a Chinese puzzle, then swings the back doors shut.

I climb into the front seat and reach for the door. Dad is holding it open, his fingers wrapping over the edge of the doorjamb.

Leaning in, he repeats the line he always uses when I am about to face the unknown, when he is letting us go, off on the first day of school or the Christmas pageants or the third-grade Springtime Jamboree that he never made it to.

"Get up there," he says. "Do a good job."

He pushes the door closed between us. "Show Billie how it's done."

Early-morning light breaks through the clouds and shines into his face. He rests his hand on top of mine, watching me.

I nod along with him, trying not to cry.

Billie is in the back with Winston and the boys, bare feet resting on the seat in front of her, headphones on. She is already a million miles away.

"Text me," I say as the van rattles beneath us and the wipers catch the last of the morning mist, set to delay. "Or call."

Jay revs the engine.

Dad nods.

He has a copy of our itinerary and all of Winston's scribbly notes in a folder on top of his dresser. I put each page through the ancient creaking copy machine down at Randy's radio station myself, just to be sure it was done right.

I know he'll never call. Dad is more a sit and wait, no news is good news kind of guy. And texting is out of the picture; his fingers are too big for his phone. I wipe my eyes, bracing myself for the good-bye.

I am cowled up in my jacket. It smells of woodsmoke and the rich tallow of meat from the night before. I lower my chin and breathe in deep, hoping that memory will stay with me a long way down the road.

Dad holds on tight for another second and then lets go, the pain of our departure already recorded and stored away for safekeeping. He watches us leave, hands jammed into his parka, the wind picking up and sweeping his dark blond hair off his forehead.

I wave as the window closes, then press my palm against the cool glass while Jay jerks us into first gear and we roll away.

12

I climb onto the stage in shadowy darkness. Our first gig on the road is in a tiny basement bar called the Rathskeller. It may be small and dark and damp, but tonight the place is packed.

I see the crowd and start unsteady, with a little wobble instead of my usual rip. Every night we will get farther from home, I think. Each night will be new, a different place, with a crowd of people ready to clap or boo or, worst of all, have no reaction at all. My fingers fumble. I'm unsure how to find my way.

I turn my back on the world and let Ty lead me in.

Focusing on his face, I lock my eyes onto his. He wipes his arm across his brow and shakes his head between beats; the pink sweatband he always wears flashes on his right forearm.

His rhythm settles into me, and I imagine we are in my

garage. It's just another Saturday night. The song is familiar, the size of the space about the same. My breathing slows as I center myself on Ty.

Billie blurs between us: boots and blond hair streaking across the tiny stage as fast as she can go.

Jay holds steady on our left with a sound so low and deep I can feel it behind my back teeth, making my throat tingle. I can't bend low enough to get to the grumble of Jay's bass guitar. I stick with Ty's bass drum instead.

Ginger Baker stands tall next to Ty, his elbow so pointy in the swampy red light, so close to the crash of Ty's cymbals. His arm cuts through the air around the drum kit like a bony sickle ending in lightning fast fingers.

Feeling grounded, I straighten my spine and turn to face the crowd. I don't need to worry if the music followed me down the road or away from home because Ty will be right behind me, note by note, all summer long.

I ratchet it up a notch, and we shake the windows down the street.

The original plan was that Billie and I would share a room. We share everything, don't we? But after a long, hot day trapped in the van, followed by a set in a tiny German basement, Ty grabs my duffel bag and swings the motel room door shut behind us.

Ty throws our bags onto the sagging double bed meant for Billie, and we drop down onto the one on the other side of the nightstand. The sleeping arrangements have changed.

The trouble is, Ty's shoulders take up too much room. I long for my skinny bed at home, the softness of my quilt. I am stuck in the crook of Ty's neck, the bleachy smell of the sheets and cheap hotel soap pressing into my nose.

I lie there for hours, flipping and flopping and sniffing the sheets until the sounds of footsteps slow in front of our door, then move on down the hall.

"Billie." Winston's voice echoes along with the soft thudding of his fists on a door. "Billie." I wait to see if she answers, scratchy sheet pulled to my chin.

"Billie." Winston thumps again.

When I sit up, Ty rolls over onto his side.

My jeans and sweater are on the floor. I pull them on and grab the room key from the dresser, then give myself the once-over in the mirror so I don't run out into the hall with a condom wrapper stuck to my foot or something.

As soon as my bare feet touch the hall carpet, I wish I had put shoes on. It is spongy.

Winston is a couple of doors down, still thudding softly. The sound of the television set blares through the closed door when I step in next to him.

"How do you know she's in there?" I ask before I start to pound along with him.

He looks pissed. "Because I'm crammed in down the hall with Ginger Baker and Jay!"

I push him out of the way with my shoulder. "Don't you have a key?"

"I didn't want to just go busting in," he says, glaring at me. "You never know what might be going on."

I hold my hand out, and Winston drops the plastic card into it. It takes me two tries; the stupid little light keeps blinking red.

"What *is* going on?" I ask as I shove the door open.

The room is lit up like the local 7-Eleven, with the curtains to the window by the parking lot window pushed open and dirty clothes tossed all over the floor. The TV is on with the sound turned all the way up.

Billie is out cold, asleep on the floor on top of a pile of lumpy hotel pillows while a fat man on TV sells knives to insomniacs at the top of his lungs.

I click it off.

"The manager called me," Winston says as he walks toward the bathroom. The exhaust fan is shaking up a storm over the tub, permanently rigged to work whenever the light is on. Winston reaches in and hits the switch. The room becomes quiet. "The neighbors got tired of the rattle."

I pull the covers back on the bed, and Winston picks Billie up from the floor. He kneels on the edge of the mattress and sets her down. She curls up on her side as soon as she touches the bed, one sock dangling from her toes.

She curled up that same way, like a cat, in the bottom of

Mom and Dad's closet right after our mom left. She'd crawl in where Mom's clothes used to hang, under the empty hangers that were clumped together and pushed into the corner, abandoned, and fall asleep.

Dad would find her when he got home. No blanket, no pillow. The single bulb above the shelf, left on to scare away any monsters, was the only thing keeping her warm.

He'd pick her up, carry her into our room, and slide her onto her bed. He'd pull the covers up under her chin and smooth her hair back as I pretended to be asleep, waiting until she was brought back to her bed, snoring and snuggly, so I could fall asleep, too.

The whole closet thing lasted about a year. My dad dropped her off each night, and then everyone but me seemed to forget about it by the next day.

I remember sitting at the kitchen table each morning before school, my cereal getting soggy, trying to figure out how she'd turned on that light. It was so high above the shelf, and the string had snapped off long ago.

Tonight the room is still bright as Winston pulls the covers up over Billie and tucks them in under her chin.

I set the extra pillows onto the bed next to her while Winston shuts the curtains. I meet him at the door with the key card in my hand. I hold it out to him and shut off the lights.

He steps past me, expecting me to stay with Billie, because

I always have. I press the key card against his chest and pull the door shut.

Winston pins the card to his shirt and shakes his head. "We're going to have to figure this out tomorrow, Teddy Lee."

I walk away, down the hall and back to Ty. Tomorrow is still a few long hours away.

"What were you thinking, Ted?" Winston asks me the next morning, as promised.

He is propped up against the outside of the roadside diner, his leg a denim kickstand covered in a trail of ash, waiting for my answer.

Honestly, I'm not thinking yet. With the door banging and the boy in my bed, I'd barely gotten any sleep last night.

The sign shaking in the wind next to the highway says BREAKFAST ALL DAY. Billie is inside, sitting in a booth facing the window and drinking a chocolate shake at 7:00 A.M. She probably slept like an angel.

She bangs on the thick glass between us, waves from the inside.

A small circle steams up the window as she leans toward it, lolling the cherry from the top of her shake around in her open mouth, coated in foamy spit and red dye number three. The cherry slips from her lips and bounces off the tabletop.

"Why?" I ask Winston, as Billie's drool dries on the Formica tabletop. "Are you worried about her?"

He looks over at me with his jaw tight, and I realize, ten years later, that it was Winston who pulled the string on the closet light for Billie.

Ty and Ginger and Jay are in a booth across the aisle from Billie, huddled around mugs of coffee that are mostly milk, pretending to be awake.

"Then you sleep with her," I say as Billie wipes her lips with the back of her hand and then sucks her shake dry in one long pull.

It is someone else's turn.

Winston glares at me and starts inside. My eyes burn with the sharp exhale of his cigarette smoke as it clouds around me. He presses his phone up against his ear and pulls the door open, probably ready to give Randy a full report.

A trucker walks up behind me, his reflection stopping next to mine in the glass. He looks in at Billie, crosses his hairy-topped arms on top of his big belly, and says, "Hell, I'll sleep with her."

I turn toward him, and he laughs and walks away.

Inside, Ty purses his lips and bends down to blow on his coffee. He looks up and finds me staring. He waves me in through the glass and I cross the crowded diner and slide into the booth by his side, leaving Billie all on her own.

Ginger listens to classical music. I know. I can hear it leaking through his headphones when he takes them off for a second. Beethoven and Bach and things like that.

I am squeezed onto the van's bench seat between him and Billie. Billie and I are playing hangman on the back of a paper place mat from the diner, and she is stealing her words from billboards as we pass.

She gives it away, her eyes glancing to the side of the road whenever it is her turn. "Steakhouse." "Rest stop." "Hot showers."

I wait for her, watching the grass waving along the sides of the freeway. It is tall and dusty green with pools of purple that disappear as it sways, pulled along by the wind and the draft of eighteen wheelers loaded with cattle and performance tires and frozen food.

I admit it, "saltwater taffy" takes me awhile. Billie bites the end of the pen and grins at me as my hangman gets feet, then hands, then a handlebar mustache. Somehow I missed that one when it rolled by.

Jay and Ty are up front, driving and navigating, while Winston leans in between the bucket seats from his spot in the middle, playing with the radio and lighting cigarettes with the dashboard lighter as the mile markers fly by.

But Ginger Baker is lost somewhere, centuries ago, his fingers twitching along on an imaginary fortepiano posing as a shag-covered bench. He is scribbling away, making brisk pencil strokes on a lined page in a leather notebook, stopping to compare it with another sheet of graph paper that he has half hidden under his long, skinny leg as he juggles a coffee in his other hand.

I am not judging his musical choice, and I am not entirely surprised by it. Classical seems like the perfect fit for Ginger. It is full of structure and purpose and feeling, but without words—just like him.

Maybe I am a little bit impressed and, okay, jealous. I can play better by ear than by reading music. If I close my eyes and listen to a song, I can knock it out with the few chords I know. If I try to read the music, it takes me awhile 'cause I can't feel it as much when my eyes are busy.

I study Ginger, wondering how what he is listening to morphs into the scribbles coming out of his hand. I wish I could climb right into his head, that I could write music the proper way, like him.

"Someday can you teach me how to do that?" I ask, staring at the sharp little notes with long winged tops stretching across the paper, ordered and systematic.

Billie crowds in, the hangman word she is working on forgotten. Her bottom lip sticks out as she examines the paper in Ginger's lap.

"Then Ty is going to teach me the guitar," she says, swaying as we change lanes.

"Why do you always have to get something if I get something?" I ask. It's like she is still five years old and we are getting chocolate bars at the grocery store.

"It's only fair."

"To who?"

Ginger watches us, silent as always. He would be an excellent secret keeper. Or spy.

"To me," Billie says. Of course, what was I thinking?

"Besides," she says, looking over at Ginger, "he didn't say yes."

She twists away, filling in the blanks below the hangman's noose, pressing hard with the ballpoint pen. "Up yours," it says, but there are three spaces left over.

"He doesn't say anything," I say, grabbing the pen.

I draw in her hangman. Crook his neck and dangle his toes. Dead.

I am afraid I bothered Ginger, botched up his brilliance somehow with my unexpected request, because he has stopped writing. I lick my lips, suddenly nervous around this innocuous boy, this quiet creature who has probably never made anyone's pulse race.

His freckles grow together as I stare too hard, watching him return to his work. He slows, deliberately drawing two big dots at the end of a staff. I know enough to know that means repeat. He looks up at me, waiting.

"Someday can you teach me how to do that?" I ask again.

He nods and turns away, never even stopping to pause his music.

※ ※ ※

In the world of music, you gotta go with who you are. And we are not Command Option Control, the techno band we are opening for. I peek out at the mostly packed tapas bar, completely unsure how and why Randy and Winston booked us this gig. Maybe we are getting paid in tacos.

With Randy tapping into his never-ending network of retired alcoholics strung across the Pacific Northwest for gigs, every night has been different: biker bars, nightclubs, house parties, bowling alleys.

Usually we don't have the time to get nervous. The van starts to shake and chatter at anything over seventy miles per hour, so most nights we walk in and we are on, practically.

It's good that way. It stops us from peeing our collective pants when we learn the headliners are a speed metal band called Black Zipper, like we did last night. Or, like tonight, when we discover my amp is blowing blue smoke again.

I twist my microphone into the stand and check out the crowd.

They all have full-on fancy square eyeglasses and bright white snug-tight T-shirts. The girls and the guys and the band itself are a mob of nearsightedness and Clorox bleach.

Last night was better.

Last night there was some flannel out there. Plus a chick with pink streaks in her hair, as well as a bunch of skinny, tattooed guys that gathered in the back. It was a good fit—a little rich, a little sweet, and some potential for damage.

But these are not our people—no flannel, no sweet. Any damage will be orderly and should be arranged for in advance. There is paperwork to be filled out at the front desk.

"Fixed," Jay announces from behind my amp.

Then he pops up and hitches up his pants.

Winston breathes a sigh of relief and lights a cigarette.

Jay is one of those guys who can fix anything. He'll sit down and stare at something and figure out how it works. My amp, the cigarette lighter in the van, Billie's miniature hair dryer: he fixed them all. While this comes in handy, it also makes me feel like I spend an inordinate amount of time with a good view of his butt crack. (FYI, boxers. Always plaid.)

Ty and Ginger are a few feet away, taping our cords to the floor.

After ten days on the road, we have begun to figure out a routine: who does what and how to get everything done that needs to get done so that we can make it onto the stage each night, reasonably close to being on time.

The guys haul the big stuff. Billie and I follow with guitars and cords and cartons of cigarettes. Ty always carries his sticks himself. Then Billie and Winston work the room, befriending bartenders and waitresses and managers while the rest of us set up, double time.

Drop that into reverse, and we are packed up at the end of the show. Cords wrapped neatly, gear stowed under the seats, people on top, and the white van rolling on toward the bitter end. We have it down.

Jay jumps off the edge of the stage and bounces over. We all huddle together, scribbling down our set list on the back of a pizza box with a big black marker Billie borrowed from the bouncer.

"The ballad killed Styx and Journey," Winston says, reading over my shoulder, as if he were some kind of sage.

I know better. Winston owns only one book, *How to Survive Anything*. He has read it cover to cover, though, so we are set if the van ever plunges into a raging river or if he gets locked inside a steamer trunk.

"Have I taught you nothing?" he calls out as he runs down the steps and retreats to his hiding place offstage.

Winston always stands to the side of the stage while we play. Beer in hand, leg jiggling along, just close enough for the waitresses to find him when he needs a refill.

"Not on purpose," I yell at the shadow now looming behind the tall speaker on my right.

Then I reach over and scratch out the Journey song anyway.

Billie stumbles toward me more than buzzed. How did she manage to get loaded while we set up? I look around for the usual suspects, skinny boys with spindly mustaches, looking completely sneaky and smoked out.

How will she win over the crowd like that?

I plug in, silently praying to the often ignored baby Jesus

for a good set, a great night, a gracious landing. Billie steps in beside me, smushing a cigarette with her foot. I don't think it was ever even lit.

"First one to miss a start has to pack the drum kit." Jay jokes as he bounces his guitar up against his hip, amped.

Ginger nods, up for the challenge.

Jay swings his guitar around to the front, ready to go.

I catch my breath right before the first few notes, just as Billie moves in close to her mic and shouts, "We are Red Velvet Crush!"

The crowd is at attention.

We tear into some serious rock music. Couples fill the dance floor, and even the most spiteful Red Velvet Crush nonbelievers are tapping their toes by the second verse. Someone, somewhere has gotten knocked up in a backseat to this song.

It brings out my inner cheerleader. She likes lip gloss and boys who play football and high kicks. I hop while Billie does the pony next to me. Her blond hair bounces up and down, her voice perfect and raspy; her breath stays even.

She spins during my solo, her skirt flaring out toward the audience, her eyes snapping onto mine after each rotation. Drunk and useless five minutes before we went on, Billie is blistering through it.

Ginger's head rolls from side to side, his eyes shut. Jay plays hard, jumping off everything he can climb. And Ty pounds under us all, a nonstop highway of snare and crash cymbals with no speed limit.

Sometimes I don't even know we are climbing until we are at the top. Sitting astride a huge wave of rhythm and energy. Sliding to the bottom on shattered fingernails and dissonance, just to start again, ready for the next ride.

How do I come down from that?

How do I go back to real life, to everyday things like history notes, hitting the snooze button at 7:00 A.M., and flossing on a regular basis?

I hold on to our final note, hoping I never have to find out. Our shoulders lift in unison, then beat down together one last time, making this great noise, this great feeling, something so much bigger than any one of us could be alone.

All sins are forgiven, all squabbles left behind. Every shred of pain and drip of sweat and stab of jealousy is worth it, over and over and over and bow.

13

Ty and I slide out of the van and spill into a parking lot as the sun starts to set behind us. I'm sure we stink. We have been on the road for more than two weeks straight, and it is summer after all.

The Laundromat has a neon sign in the window. A string of glowing pink bubbles, popping as they light up from bottom to top. The last one is broken. Ty drags our two bags of dirty laundry up over the curb, and I bring my guitar.

"Please don't tell me we got paid in quarters again," he says as I hold the glass door open for him.

"Nope," I say, flashing a ten-dollar bill. "We're big time."

The Laundromat is empty. No people, only the swishing of soapy water and the smell of softener. A good sign, I guess.

It means that at least we can leave our stuff here while it spins and soaks.

I shake my clothes out onto a table and start sorting. Ty skips that step and stuffs all of his into one machine. He gets quarters and two tiny boxes of soap from the dispenser on the wall while I select my temperatures and water levels.

Studying my piles of pinks, whites, and dirty jeans, he smiles skeptically and holds out a handful of change.

"I'm hoping for more than a lump of gray at the end," I say.

"Optimistic."

He leans in and kisses me after I drop the lid on my load of darks.

"Do you want to start on that one from last night?" he asks.

"Yeah."

I add soap while he runs to the van for Jay's acoustic bass.

Settling in, I open my guitar case and sit in the middle of a row of plastic chairs shaped like eggshells. I pull my notebook from the bottom of my bag.

Ty chooses the eggshell on the end of the row. I put the notebook on the empty seat between us as he tunes the bass, twisting his fingers and tipping his head until the sound is just right.

"It's about a girl and the pull of the moon, right?" he asks, remembering like he always does.

Our eyes meet, I nod, and we start to play. My fingers trip along, working out the melody, finding the notes that fit what Ty is thumbing out as the words from my notebook drift in my head, finally falling into place.

We started working together five nights ago after a long, late gig. Ty was taking a shower. We usually stayed in after our shows; after-parties and closing down the bar don't work for Ty. Nothing was on TV but dog races, and I had already tried home, leaving another message for my dad, again.

After the beep I breathed out, "Hi. Hope you're good." Pause. "Billie had pancakes for breakfast today, with a side order of pancakes . . . I'll send you a picture." Pause. "Okay. Miss you. Bye."

I found a picture of Billie's breakfast, a half-eaten short stack of pancakes, swimming in a brown sea of syrup, and hit send.

Picturing Dad at the kitchen table alone, a full box of bran flakes in front of him, or watching TV until he fell asleep every night in a dark and empty house made me feel sad, so I pulled out my notebook and my guitar.

My fingers hadn't tightened up yet, so it wasn't hard to slip right back in and get lost in my own world. I was singing to myself when I realized that Ty was behind me, a towel wrapped around his waist, humming along.

"You were so far away," he said quietly.

He sat down next to me and reached for my notebook,

drawing five wobbly horizontal lines across the page, followed by a lot of notes.

"What are you doing?" I asked.

He didn't look up.

"Arranging," he said.

He grabbed his sticks and pounded out a rhythm on the corner of the mattress. It sounded good. I didn't get how he did it; but I liked it anyway.

"What comes next?" he asked, urging me on.

I played, and he scribbled down notes, adding structure underneath my melody and smoothing it all out into a song.

We backed up over a tricky part, and he sat down next to me.

"Someday," he said, "somebody else should hear this."

"You sure?" I asked because that was what I wanted. Someone who got me, who made me feel connected and cared for, but knew when I needed a nudge, even if that scared the crap out of me.

"Absolutely," he said, but his smile sold me.

We have been working together every night since, superlate after a show or first thing in the morning, wrapped up in the sheets of some unknown hotel, setting my words to music.

Ty finds an all-night diner or nonstop convenience store and stocks up on blue slurpees and chocolate cake, and then, covered in cake crumbs, we play into the wee hours, stopping occasionally to make out like blue-tongued zombies until the sun comes up.

I strum one more time tonight and stop. I've gotten as far as I can go. I'm out of words.

"How does it end?" Ty asks, playing a low, rambling bass line that I can feel through the seats.

I look at him and shrug.

We are together, surrounded by suds and hum. I am warm and safe, and it smells like soap. I don't ever want this one to end.

"Well, then," Ty says, continuing to play, "let's just tumble."

"Would you look at that?" Jay drops his duffel in front of the van, claps his hands above his head, and then vaults over the waist-high chain-link fence in front of the motel pool. It is tiny and covered in cracked blue tile, but definitely swimmable.

The motel surrounds the pool on three sides, the parking lot on the other. Two wood-shingled floors with an Astroturf-covered balcony run the length of the motel's second floor, cutting sharp corners to cap the ends of the pool with staircases.

"Our first pool." Billie smiles as Jay pulls the gate open for her from the inside. She heaves her backpack up against the fence, sits right down on the cement, and pulls off a boot.

"Don't anybody drown," Winston says, heading off toward the office.

I follow along behind him. Winston always drags me with him for administrative tasks such as checking in, ordering food, and paying for broken and/or missing items. Jay is officially hyperactive, Ty is too easily distracted, and Billie is, well, Billie, so Winston appointed me. Ginger Baker is probably more responsible than all of us put together, but it is hard to be certain since he never actually speaks.

"Winston Carter?" The little round man behind the desk reads Winston's name aloud and upside down, breaking each syllable into pieces as Winston fills in his info and the van's plate number on the required form. The man is kind of red and meat colored, like a ham.

Winston stops writing and nods.

Hambone breathes heavily.

"Well, Mr. Carter . . . that'll be two hundred thirty-nine dollars and ninety-six cents, not including incidentals." He rocks back on his heels as if he thinks we can't cover it.

I make a mental note to make sure that Billie steals nothing bigger than a bar of soap. Country ham looks like a stickler.

Winston whips a wad of Randy's cash out of his front pocket, and the guy's eyes bulge. Winston flips through the bills and hands over five of them.

"We're old school," he says to the clerk with a forced

smile as he reaches into his other pocket to grab his chiming phone.

He checks a text and hands his phone to me.

It's from Randy. We are canceled for tonight.

Winston stuffs his phone back into his jacket and starts to light a cigarette.

Hambone shakes his head and points dramatically at the no smoking sign posted on the paneled wall next to Winston's head.

Winston slides out the door in a puff of nicotine as the little man scowls. He straightens some papers on his desk, regaining his composure. He hands me our change, which I pocket, and then drops four metal room keys into my open hand.

Each one has a flat green plastic diamond attached to it that is engraved with the room number. Talk about old school.

"Office closes at ten," he says to me in a clipped voice as he glares at the growing cloud of smoke swirling outside his office door.

He rotates and then gulps for air before he walks away and disappears into a room no bigger than a glorified closet to plop down in front of a tiny TV, our business finished.

Billie is sitting at the edge of the pool, feet submerged, leaning up against a metal ladder in her undies and a T-shirt when Winston and I get back. Her boots are dumped at the end of a woven plastic chaise lounge, and the bruises on her skinny legs look fresh and blue. She probably bumped into something onstage last night.

Ginger Baker is stretched out on a lounge chair, arms over his head, apparently asleep, his body as limber as a wooden clothespin.

"We're canceled for tonight," Winston says.

Ty sneaks up from behind, wraps his arms around my waist, and says, softly over my shoulder, "An entire day off."

"An entire day without money," Winston replies.

"No problem," Ty says like it is no big deal. And it isn't for him. He can always get money from home.

"At least there's a pool," Billie says.

"Yeah, the last place didn't even have a bathtub," Jay remarks.

"Sorry, Queen Victoria," Winston says. He doesn't look up; he is busy tapping another cigarette out of his pack.

"I like to soak," Jay says as he spins himself around, trapped inside a tiny, lime green inner tube with a dinosaur head on it. Some kid, somewhere, is driving away in a packed station wagon, missing that thing.

"Are any of them poolside?" Jay asks.

I look at the keys in my hand and the numbers on the doors.

"One," I say.

We moved to a four-room system after that first night

when Billie slept alone and Winston learned that he does not like to share. I'm willing to bet the money for the extra room doesn't come out of his cut.

Jay points to Ginger and yells, "My man!" like this is the Four Seasons in Maui and Ginger is in any way excitable.

I smile. I like that about Jay. For a sorta rich boy, he can slum it up with the rest of us and somehow be psyched about it.

"Was it us?" Ty asks Winston.

Winston shrugs and inhales, "Headliner probably couldn't sell out the club."

"Hell, we could sell out a club."

Jay twirls again, dragging a beer can in his wake.

Winston smiles. "Someday."

He picks through the keys in my hand, pulls out the one marked 204, and makes his way to the open wooden stairs heading up to the second floor.

Winston is not going to swim. I'm not sure I've ever even seen his legs.

"You know what we need?" Ty asks out of the blue.

He peels off his T-shirt and tosses it at a chair.

"More time spent in daylight?" I ask.

Everyone is so white. Except Ginger; he goes way past white into a world of translucent. Only his hair has color.

Ty loses his shoes and socks in a pile and then backs up to the fence. He runs at the water, knowing we all are waiting to hear what he is going to say. He lifts into a dive as soon as his toes hit the words NO DIVING painted in red letters on the deck.

"Fried chicken?" Billie shouts right before his pointed hands split the water open. Her ankles glow white, rippling in his wash.

Ty comes up shaking his head.

"No, not chicken." He pauses, breathing, shoulder deep.

"New songs," he says with a triumphant grin.

My heart skips. This is not a nudge. This is a push right into the deep end. A dunk. And I'm not even holding my breath.

"Awesome!" Jay says. "I was only thinking of floating beer cozies."

Ginger leans up on one elbow and looks at me.

Ty's words just sit there. Everyone heard him. Are they waiting for it to sink in?

"New songs. Really?" Jay asks.

"Yeah, don't you think?"

"To the songs, not the chicken?" Jay clarifies, his brain seemingly scrambled by excitement.

Ty nods.

"Shouldn't Winston be here?" Jay asks.

"He's not in the band," Billie says. She pulls her dripping ankles from the water. "Technically."

"If we're discussing this, I mean," Jay says.

He tries to spin in his tube, but it turns into a splash.

Ty holds on to the edge of the pool, leans his head back, and yells toward the balcony overlooking the pool. "Winston!"

"Is this a meeting then?" Jay asks, paddling his way toward the deep end.

"No, no. Not really," Ty says, glancing up at me.

I stand silently. A dark cloud blocking out the sun.

"Feels like one," Billie says, leaning back, the palms of her hands flat on the cement.

Ty pulls himself from the water on the far side of the pool. His back muscles flex once, strong, and then he is out.

"It's just . . . . up for discussion," he turns and says.

I watch him drip.

"I don't want to discuss this at all," I say to him.

The songs are mine. And I thought they were just between the two of us, at least until I was ready. Looks like I am wrong.

I step over to the nearest table. It has a crooked umbrella and a white rubber ring around the edge, the acrylic surface covered in cigarette burns and scratch marks. I drop two room keys on it.

"What's with TL?" Jay asks as I walk away.

Ty doesn't answer.

The remaining room key digs into my hand as I hit each wooden step, hard, and pray I didn't manage to walk away with the one poolside key. I didn't think to check the room number, and there is no way I am going back down there. Not now.

"Wait," Billie asks from below. "She's TL now?"

"Don't worry about it, Billie," Ty says; then he yells up again from the pool. "Winston!"

The door to room 204 swings open next to me. Winston stands there: no shirt, just jeans, white feet, and a can of beer.

"Are we on fire?" he asks.

"No. Ty is just being stupid."

"Well, drummers are strange people," Winston says.

He grabs his T-shirt from the dresser top just inside the door and pulls it on over his head.

"Get down here, man!" Jay is yelling this time.

Winston shrugs at me like "Well, what you gonna do?" and pulls his door shut to brush past me.

I finally look down at the key in my hand. 208. Billie will be between us.

I stick the key in the door and wiggle it, glancing down at the pool. Ginger is watching me.

Jay paddles over to the edge of pool as Winston walks toward it.

"I need your lighter," Jay says.

Winston tosses it to him casually, the way boys do, not even worrying that it might get wet, and sits down under the crooked umbrella. Ty thumps back into the pool, doing a cannonball that drenches Billie and the surrounding cement.

I step inside my room and stop, leaving the door open a crack, waiting, the conversation from the pool drifting in with the breeze, wiping out the tired smell of carpet freshener and long-haul truckers.

But there is no more talk about new songs, just the click of the lighter, the splash of the pool, and Billie's giggles. My songs are forgotten.

That kind of bothers me, but kind of not. When Ginger finally stretches back out and closes his eyes, I shut the door.

My last note is settling in over our hotel room that night when Ty walks in. I have the blackout curtains drawn, the lamps glowing, the plastic ice bucket filled with melting ice that I have no use for.

Ty crawls in behind me and lies flat on the bed, staring up at the ceiling. I set my guitar next to him.

"Beautiful," he says. "All your songs, they're beautiful, you know."

My breath catches in my throat, and I turn toward him.

"I don't disbelieve that," I say.

"But?"

But I thought he would be more careful. I thought he would know how much my songs mean to me, without my ever having to say it.

"But I can't let Billie have everything," I say.

"But it's not just for Billie. It's for the band."

"I will not be demoted to singing harmony," I say. "Not for these."

Ty rolls onto his side, props his head on his hand, and looks at me.

"What?" I ask. "I should just stand there, ooohing and aaahing to songs I have written?"

I cross my arms and look down at him. He doesn't understand. Ty is an only child. He doesn't know the hate and love and entanglement that come along with a sister like Billie. He doesn't see the burden and promise of it, the weight of being connected to someone in a way that can never be cut.

He doesn't feel the strength that it takes to keep her even at arm's length when it would be so much easier to give in and give her everything, to light the way for her and lose myself completely, until I am nothing but Billie's heavy conscience, Billie's bad habits, Billie's broken heart.

He reaches up and pulls me down next to him. Smooths my hair across my forehead and tucks it behind my ear.

"Trust me?" he asks.

I roll onto my back and let my arms fall flat.

When does a crush turn to love? Officially? When you've slept together a couple of times? Eaten breakfast, lunch, and dinner together all in the same day? Seen each other pee? How do you let go of the fear of falling and just fall? Not fearing the bottom or the inevitable crash? I am there, dangling.

I nod. Maybe this is what faith is supposed to feel like.

Ty breathes out. He smiles down at me as I turn over and slip under him, angled in and protected, tucked into a warm cove of muscles and the spicy smell of Speed Stick.

14

Led Zeppelin wakes me up. I open my eyes wide and look out the van window. The sky above us is thin and blue with clouds that crack like desert sand. Where exactly are we?

The highway rolls by, flat and black. Scrubby little bushes dot its edge. There are hills in the distance, probably covered in scrubby little bushes, too.

Billie is curled up next to me. Her chin rests on her arm along the back of the bench as she stares out the side window. Her eyes move as we pass mile marker 252.

Ginger is driving, and Jay is manning the passenger seat up front. Jay has all of his gadgets—his phone, his extra GPS, and his laptop—spread out on the dash in front of him, at the ready for any detour or wrong turn or a possible career in espionage.

Ty is out cold in the backseat, sitting up with his arms crossed over his chest and his legs stretched out in front of him so far that they almost look as long as Winston's, who has been demoted to the backseat for once.

When I pictured us on the road, I thought only about the good stuff. I thought about the jokes, the time spent together, the fun and adventure and new sights and places. I thought it was going to be a never-ending joyride on carpeted seats.

I didn't think about the absolute boredom, the oh my God, if I have to sit next to you and listen to you breathe for even just one more hour, I might have to kill you moments.

I didn't think about the in-between places like this, where there are no radio stations at all, unless you love country or have religious fervor. I grew tired of everything every one of us had brought along days ago—especially Winston's classic rock collection. It took only about four weeks on the road for those songs to wear thin.

I didn't think all the new sights and places would be parking lots and gas stations and holding your breath in rest stop bathrooms—or holding it until the next stop altogether. Which is always just another gas station, because boys never have to go. Even after a jumbo soda and a cup of coffee.

"Do we need to stop?" Ty asked hours ago as we blew by another way station at sixty-five miles per hour.

"I'm fine," Winston said. "You?"

"Fine," Jay said over his shoulder. "You?"

Ginger gave the thumbs-up. He was fine.

Jay checked the GPS, and Ginger took the van to a shaky seventy miles per hour, and I fell asleep with my legs crossed.

I didn't think about how Billie would spit a wad of gum out of the window one day, and it would be so hot and windy outside that it would blow back in and land next to me, a sticky bright pink wad stuck to the carpeted seats.

Staring at it now makes me hungry.

"Where are the snacks?" I ask, digging for the wrinkled paper bag that usually holds our stash of chips and soda.

"This is all we have left," Winston says, tossing two packs of cheese and peanut butter crackers at me.

"Don't they set rat traps with these?" I ask.

They are fluorescent orange with an industrial sealant brown filling.

"It's possible," he says, tearing his pack open with his teeth.

Like a rat, I think.

I didn't think that sometimes it would feel like this is just mile after mile and gig after gig, piling one on top of another, layering up like a soft mountain of ash.

"I'm not so sure a night off was a good thing," Winston says, chewing his crackers and watching me rub the second set of carpet wrinkles of the day from the side of my face.

We hit a bump in the road, a pothole or something that makes the fake crown swing from the rearview mirror. Jay holds his hands up, protecting his gadgetry, while he gives Ginger a nasty sidelong glance.

Ty finally stirs. He stretches his arms out and flexes his fingers.

He opens his eyes and winces.

"Is it always going to smell like french fries in here?" he asks.

He drops his arms.

"I told you not to let her eat in the car," I say, looking at Billie.

Somehow Billie dropped an order of fries—not just one or two but an entire small paper sleeve full—behind the shag bench two days ago. Now every time it heats up inside the van even a little bit, it smells like a deep-fat fryer.

Jay tried to fish them out with a long screwdriver, but it didn't fit into the crack. He wanted to disassemble the whole bench, his eyes measuring and hungry, but Winston said we didn't have the time.

How the fries made it down into that crack was a mystery to all of us, including Billie. It was like the van was hungry that day.

Oddly enough, the wad of Billie's gum landed right where the fries live. The smell is strongest there, almost directly under Billie.

"She's a food nuisance," I say.

My car has enough broken corn chips and straw wrappers

stuck under the passenger seat to attest to this fact. No jury or deliberation necessary.

"So says the girl who orders her cheeseburgers well done," Winston says.

He leans over and cracks the triangular window next to him.

"I like things a bit roached." I shrug. No big deal.

Winston tsks at me and flicks his ash out the window.

"It's a shameful waste of perfectly good meat," he says.

He turns toward Ty, and they bow at each other, like two warriors having defeated an enemy in a kung fu movie. Medium rare: 2. Well done: 0.

"Are we talking about dinner?" Jay turns around and asks.

Eat. Meat. They do sound the same. But he probably thinks he missed out on a high-five opportunity and feels the need to jump in.

I check my phone.

"It's only two-fifteen," I say.

Jay reaches back and turns the radio down. He's rigged his iPad into the antique dashboard. Robert Plant only whispers to me now about cloaks and clocks and threads with no end.

"Late lunch?" he asks.

"I don't care what you eat," Winston replies, "but Teddy Lee and Billie only get fifteen bucks for the day."

Normally Winston buys everything with Marlboro points. His future lung cancer is sponsored. He has the duffel bag (seventy-five points), the shot glass set (fifty points), even the baseball cap (sixty-five points) to prove it. He's not used to having actual money, and it turns out he is quite tightfisted.

"Does that include beer money?" Jay asks.

Winston nods.

Jay reaches into his front pocket and pulls out a crumple of bills. He picks some pocket fuzz out from the wrinkled money and lets it drift down into the carpet to join forces with the seventies shag.

He smooths and counts, then twists back toward us with a grin.

"Lunch it is then," he says.

Ginger Baker eats with a knife and fork, British style. I've seen it dozens of times by now, but it still makes me want to dress him in a little suit with shorts and a striped tie and send him off to school.

His egg, sunny side up, splits open and oozes yellow. He has very long fingers. Nice nails. Not ragged and bitten like Jay's. Jay is so impatient he can't even wait for his nails to grow. He chews them off before they get a chance.

I stare at Ginger's hands, trying to ignore the paper next to Ty's plate, its torn edges, the words that are coming at me.

"Just let Ginger take a look," Ty says, reaching over to slide the paper toward Ginger. "I let him in on what we've been up to," he tells me.

I am sandwiched in a booth between Ty and Ginger, my Monte Cristo growing cold, the cheese becoming sweaty and solid. Jay and Winston and Billie are outside, leaning up against a car the color of lipstick, smoking.

The paper between us is filled with my curved words and Ty's straight lines, a song we have been working on during one of our late-night sessions. "Which one is it?" I ask, avoiding his eyes and the new hole in my heart, a sore, empty spot that didn't exist before that day at the pool.

I can't be mad at Ginger about this. That would be like thinking that Mozart was going to wreck your musical career. Ty knows that, so I've been outmaneuvered.

"It's the one about making out in the morning," Ty says, sliding the page toward Ginger.

It does say that, scrawled in the upper corner. Ty is smart. It is one of my favorites. Ginger pulls the paper closer to him and slides a pencil out of his jacket pocket. He scans the page and starts penciling notes, intense and fast. Squinting, I try to read as he writes. I swear, with that handwriting Ginger should be a doctor. His first procedure should be fixing my wobbly, bruised heart.

Ginger sets the paper back down by my plate. I stare at the sharp, slanted notes that somehow stack together and make one of my songs better.

I nudge it away with my fingertips and look past the dirty plates lining the other side of the booth, past where Billie has dragged her finger through a puddle of ketchup, past the dregs of Winston's chocolate milk, up to the gray summer sky outside the window.

There is more to playing my songs than the feeling that I am laying myself out flat for all the world to see or opening myself up and sharing what has been, until recently, all mine. There is Billie and how they will break her, because if we are really going to do this, I want to sing.

I sigh.

"You know I don't know how to do that." I remind Ty, tapping the page on top of a skinny bass clef.

"Ginger'll help you," he mumbles, his mouth full of burger, medium rare.

On my other side, Ginger is tucking toast points away at an alarming rate. He nods in agreement.

"And we'll need to practice," I say, my brain skipping ahead to the logistics and the space and the little details everyone else will forget.

Ty pushes his plate away knowing he has won.

"Jay is going to be so stoked!" He pounds a rhythm into the edge of the table that makes Ginger's eggs wiggle. "Soon we won't have to be a cover band anymore!"

"Billie should start memorizing lyrics now." He continues, looking out the window as Winston and Jay and Billie weave their way back across the parking lot, a tepee of cigarette butts left behind them.

"No, I want to sing," I say, breaking the news in one big breath.

Ginger's fork freezes midair.

"You're sure?" Ty asks, leaning in close with his eyebrows raised.

I nod. "For these, for sure."

Ty squeezes me tight, bumping me up against Ginger Baker in his excitement.

"It's gonna be *so* good," he says, his voice as close to a squeal as a boy with arms like cannons can get.

"Yeah." I laugh and untangle myself, saving the best for last. "But now you're gonna have to teach Billie how to play the guitar."

Ginger smiles and raises his coffee mug, ready to seal the deal. I raise mine. Ty watches us suspiciously, shrugs, and then raises his, too. Clink.

For the past four mornings Ty has begged or borrowed or scammed a small meeting room in each of our hotels for the three of us to practice in.

Today's is called the Sunrise Room. A small easel stands on silver legs outside the doors announcing the big event: Marketing Concepts—Luncheon at Noon. We promised to be out by ten.

The carpet is dark blue with a tiny diamond pattern, and the tan walls are sectioned, so you can fold them up and roll them away, making an even bigger Sunrise Room if you need one. I'm not much for navigation, but I am pretty sure you can't see the sunrise from anywhere in here. Small or large, the room faces the wrong direction.

We plug in but keep it low. So far we have been working on arrangements, piecing the songs together. Today I am going to sing for the two of them for the first time. Nerves are shooting through me: little bolts that make me trip over my guitar cord and drop my pick for the third time.

I stand up and hear Ty say, "Ta-ta-tee-tee-ta," and suddenly I am last chair in the fifth-grade band again.

"Ta-ta-tee-tee-ta," Mr. Beauregard said back then, and I scowled as he poised his arms in the air, readying us.

My feet dangled from a folding chair. The clarinet, the lamest of all instruments, rested between my legs.

Just count it off, I thought. That was what I had learned in my guitar book.

Mr. B was a sweaty pork rind of a man. His stomach bulged over the waistband of his pants while he swung that useless little conductor stick in the air endlessly, like any of us were watching.

We were eleven. It was the first day of school, and some of us weren't even sure how to hold our borrowed or rented instruments, let alone play them, and he was up there, saying ta-ta-tee-tee-ta like we were the goddamn philharmonic. I couldn't decide if that was severe optimism or complete ignorance. I quit band the next day.

But when Ty moves his fingers along in the air on an invisible fiddle or viola or something and says, "Bum-de-bum-de–bum-de-beyeeeooowww," Ginger nods, completely fluent in the secret language of music geeks and middle school band teachers that eludes me.

Seconds later they are bouncing along and I am struggling to keep up.

How can Ginger already be better at my own songs than I am?

It's true: he is a musical genius. Ta-ta-totally. I watch his fingers fly and miss my cue to sing.

I drop my shoulders and shake my head. I've been here before, once in the garage when I tried to sing for the first time and again right now. Unfortunately I crashed and burned both times.

Ty and Ginger loop back around, playing me in. I have to jump. Now.

All the air is knocked out of my gut. I pump the dry squeeze box that is my abdomen and push the first note out of my mouth. It is good. Not as smoky and sweet as Billie, but damn good.

Distracting my shaky stomach with my fingering, I tap out the beat with my toes. I hold tight to my guitar, slowing my voice so it doesn't run away from me. My palms are sweaty. Fireworks burst inside my brain: I did it! I'm doing it! Keep doing it!

Ty smiles, and Ginger nods along.

I ease into the pocket and even out my breathing, my voice rising high into the open Sunrise Room, like liquid sunshine.

My heart is still pounding when the song ends. My fingers flutter along the neck of my guitar, even though I'm not playing a note. I feel like I am in a dream.

I hear clapping, but it is far away, muted and fuzzy. Ty and Ginger are beaming at me, but their hands aren't moving. The clapping gets louder.

Ty turns toward the door. Ginger sets his guitar down.

Billie is standing in the doorway wearing striped pajama pants and an Oregon Ducks sweatshirt. She has half a bagel held between her front teeth as she slowly claps. Why did Winston wait until today to finally score us a hotel with a breakfast bar?

She stops clapping and slowly takes us in: the three guitars, the cups of coffee, the notes and papers resting on the chairs behind us.

How did I think this was going to happen?

Did I think we were just going to spring it on her one night? Stand back, Billie, we've got a song that you won't be singing.

Now that she is here, I felt better, less guilty, because at least now she knows. Now all I have to do is clean up the mess.

Billie looks past Ty to the windows that span the side of the Sunrise Room. Right behind Ginger there is a scenic view of the parking lot.

She takes a bite of the bagel and says, as if she doesn't give a shit about what we are doing, "So there's no pool?"

Billie doesn't answer when I knock on her door. It is wedged open, so I push my way in, wondering if she slept that way, with the door open, cracked enough to let light in from the hall.

I kick a crumpled matchbook cover from under the door and listen for the latch to click behind me. Once my eyes adjust to the darkness of the room, I climb into the bed, across a jumble of sheets and hotel pillows and slide under the slippery bedspread.

Billie is buried near the bottom, curled up with the remote tucked under her chin, watching as cartoons play silently on the TV five feet away. It feels like I haven't really seen her for so long. Her fingernails are chewed short, and it looks like one cuticle is bleeding. We both have faded X's on our hands, left over from last night.

"Too young to drink, but old enough to rock your world," a guy with a mustache and way too many muscles said to his skinnier friend when they walked by Billie and me as we were setting up.

"We should get that printed on a T-shirt." Billie laughed, wrapping her microphone cord around her fingers and watching the muscleman go.

Today her hair is shiny and blown out superstraight,

fanning out around her head on the pillow. She is fully dressed, covered head to toe in bright pink, even her lips, but the bottoms of her feet are black and bare.

I picture her padding around in the hotel hallway at all hours, perfect from the ankles up.

Our mom was the same way. Hair perfect. Lipstick on. Shoes left behind.

In first grade she showed up at my school one day with a squished sandwich in a wrinkled paper bag. And maybe some leftover pie from the restaurant—Marionberry, I bet.

"Teddy, Teddy Lee," she whispered to me from the hall, followed by the wrinkling of the bag.

I looked up from my spelling book. So did the entire class, including Mr. K, the best teacher ever. My fingers gripped the edge of my avocado green desk. I was frozen.

Mom stood in her waitress uniform and the suntan pantyhose she got at the drugstore. Her hair was done up, her lipstick applied and blotted, but she had slippers on her feet. I gripped my desk even tighter.

I glanced up at Mr. K, wondering if I should answer her. He ran a pretty tight ship.

In the end I stayed put.

Mr. K walked over and retrieved my wrinkled lunch, which he slid into the little wire basket under my seat, while I stared down at my spelling book until I heard those slippers slipping away.

I wriggle in, really close, and Billie stirs. She sets the remote down and looks me in the eyes. I watch her brow furrow, her lips pouting as an idea becomes a thought and the thought becomes words.

"Soon all the songs will be yours," she says, staring past me.

Over her shoulder I watch a cat hit a mouse in the head with a hammer. I exhale and smooth out the small spot of empty sheet beneath us.

"Don't you think we're pretty far away from that?" I ask.

Billie shrugs, but we are. We are *so* far away from that.

Can't we wait until I can play at least one of my own songs well before we all start to worry? Besides, Jay and Winston are barely in on it yet.

"You know it sucks for me, right?" Billie asks.

I do. I want to pretend that it doesn't matter, but I can see it—in her eyes, in her skinny shoulders, in the quiver when she speaks.

"Yeah." I nod.

She picks at her nails and keeps quiet, being very serious and un-Billie for a few minutes.

When she finally squirms and says, "That guitar makes my fingers hurt," I know we are back to regular Billie.

Ty is teaching her how to play. He ran out and bought her a brand-new guitar, keeping up his end of the deal that Ginger and I made.

It was waiting for her in the front seat of the van when we packed up to leave the afternoon I told Ty and Ginger I wanted to sing. She never even asked why. It had pink sparkles on it, and that was enough.

I reach over and examine her fingers. The tips are red but not raw.

"Are you scared?" I ask.

She shakes her head.

I know she wants to believe that we are always thinking and feeling the same thing.

When we were little, she would suddenly look over and ask me with her eyes lit up, "Are you thinking what I'm thinking?" She wished we were wonder twins, with great hair and boots and telepathic powers.

I studied her. Tried to mind meld. But I always gave in.

"I don't know," I'd say. "What are you thinking?"

This time I know better. I loop my fingers around hers.

This time I say, "Me, too."

15

We are pulling into Pocatello, into that endless gray light that can somehow seem much brighter than sunshine, even if it's just seconds from flat-out rain. I watch a freeway interchange coming up, a concrete cloverleaf of double yellow lines and hybrid cars. My eyes dilate in the bright light and then throb.

Everyone inside the van seems as listless as the weather. Maybe nobody's born to be wild when it's overcast, but come on. We are the farthest away from home we will get on this trip, the farthest away I have ever been. They can at least act excited.

Plus, tomorrow night I will sing for the first time. We will use tonight to feel out the crowd for original material. I am hiding my nervousness under a hoodie, a jean jacket, and a vow of silence, Ginger Baker style. Thank God for one more night.

"Okay, here's the deal," Winston calls out from the driver's seat in his loud DJ school voice as he stops the van. "We've booked two nights with a band called"—short pause while he consults his managerial clipboard—"Blasting Cap."

"Woohoo." Billie claps, half assed.

"Cool name," Jay says, coming alive, stretching his arms toward the carpeted sky and yawning big.

Ty nods. "Wish I would have thought of that."

"Our name is cool," Jay says.

"It is, in an Elvis's grandmother's favorite cake recipe kind of way." Ty jokes, stabbing me through the heart with his words.

"I love cake," Jay says, so dreamy and wanton that I seriously question if I have fallen for the wrong former Trigger Brother.

Winston consults the top sheet on his stack of papers and peers out the side window. "This has got to be it."

He drops his clipboard onto the dash and slowly eases the van into the entrance. The back end creaks up and over the curb into the parking lot. A bum stands next to a pink rosebush under a weathered marquee that says THE BARRACUDA LOUNGE.

TONIGHT BLASTING CaP!

I sit back in my seat. They couldn't spring for another big *A*?

The sky is getting darker, dimming down to rain. We circle the empty parking lot, doing our usual drive by.

The homeless guy slides behind the rosebush when we make our way around to the front of the building again. The van lurches over the curb and out into the empty street, leaving him behind.

It starts to sprinkle. Winston snaps the headlights on, lighting up the pink, red, and yellow rosebushes that line the streets. The roses glow from the misty background. We follow their colors down the rain-washed streets, all the way downtown and to our hotel with a capital H.

Yep, this one has more than two floors.

Winston dumps us out at the front doors and goes to park the van. The Hotel has a swanky old-time lobby with a velvet sofa and a dusty smell. It may be tall and stately, but nice left this hotel a long time ago. Timeworn is the best way to describe it. I get in line to check in while Billie and the boys crash on the sofa in the corner.

I'm behind a tiny, pale guy with slick black hair. Skinny arms. Twenty-two at best, he appears to be turning hotel registration into some sort of Advanced Placement test.

"We're in a band," he says to me over his shoulder, as if he were apologizing and trying to impress me at the same time.

It does explain the knot of dark-haired smokers in the other corner staring at us.

I nod. "That's nice."

He folds up his paperwork and slides it into the inside pocket of his vest. Then he turns and looks me up and down.

I try to ignore the fact he has no shirt on, just the vest. Eww. Finally he steps to the side, letting me at the front desk.

"Wait," dark and tiny says, shaking his head. "That usually works."

The girl behind the counter smiles at me past her lip piercing.

"We have a reservation," I say to her. "Carter. Red Velvet Crush?"

I'm not sure how Randy made the reservation.

"You're the Crush?" my new little friend asks.

"Apparently."

"Good name. Very dramatic." He raises his arm with a flourish of black polished fingertips. "We're your headliner, Blasting Cap."

He points his finger at me and shoots an imaginary pistol when he says the band's name, but I doubt this guy could handle a BB gun, let alone a serious weapon of any kind.

I fill out the van's info and forge Winston's signature on the receipt.

He continues. "We're only slumming here until we swing on through to Seattle."

I nod. "Sweet."

He lifts his chin toward the scrum of greasy rock boys in the corner.

"That's the band," he says as they stub out their cigarettes and make their way across the faded carpet toward us. They all are dark and small just like him, but he is obviously the master of ceremonies.

They nod. The one closest to me has tragically bad teeth. I watch him smile and thank God that Billie, Winston, and I were lucky enough to end up with good teeth. Lord knows we can't afford the dentist. Most days I am glad we have enough toothpaste to go around.

"That's my band." I lift my chin toward the sofa.

"Yours?"

"Yep."

"And the little blonde?" the cutest one asks.

Billie is squealing and laughing as Ty puts her into a headlock and Jay messes up her hair.

"That's Billie," I say.

I gather up the key cards in their little envelopes and the printed map of the hotel with our rooms circled in black ink.

They all are watching Billie, but I'm not worried. They are nothing more than a flea circus for Billie to train for her entertainment and eventually swat away.

"Don't bother," I say as I walk away with my hands full, "she won't remember your name tomorrow."

"We can live with that." The ringmaster chuckles. "And by the way," he calls after me, "it's Ben."

"There are way more dudes out there than last night," one of the Blasting Caps boys says as I squeeze by behind him and stop, scanning the room for Billie. He is blocking his dressing room doorway so he can peek out at the crowd. It is almost a full house.

This is a big club. Not just for us, but for any band. It has a real backstage, with separate dressing rooms for Blasting Cap and us. Their room is bigger, full of cast-off furniture and an old oak bar and tons of people.

THE BAND is painted above their doorway, and someone drew a skinny rocker dude in a wifebeater and big boots on the wall next to the door; the grubby light switch is his belly button.

We are definitely riding on Blasting Cap's coattails. They bring a crowd with them, and I am nervous and anxious to sing to a full room, an excited mob. But I need to find Billie first. I tell myself I will worry about singing after that. The thought makes my throat dry up.

I spy Billie in the darkest corner, making out with one of the Blasting Cap boys with reckless abandon. I hope it's the cute one. They are kissing like they can't be seen, like they aren't backstage, surrounded by strangers and assorted musical instruments. It makes my tongue tired just watching.

"Where are all the hot chicks?" the first Cap moans.

He has gray jeans on with silver designs sewn into the back pockets and tattooed arms. His jeans hang low on his skinny ass as he turns back into the room and presses himself against the wall that separates the stage from backstage.

"All those dudes out there greatly decrease our chances of getting laid, you know." He drops into a chair in a puff of Old Gold dust.

"Are you kidding?" the other one asks, his eyes sliding over to Billie in the corner, "What if she brought along some friends? Can you imagine?"

Then he takes his turn peeking out at the club.

"Way worth the extra dudes."

The first one—shiny pants—sighs. "I do love the crazy ones."

"We all do." The second one agrees as they tap their beer bottles together, toasting my little sister and her supposed legion of hot friends.

I probably should be offended. But I laugh and pass them by, knowing that Billie's never really had any friends. Temporary tattoos last longer.

Blasting Cap showed up super-early to our sound check, arriving backstage with fresh bottles of booze and dusty red packets of bottle rockets while Ty and Jay were double-checking our gear and retaping our cords to the floor. The two of them walk up next to me now, their eyes flicking toward Billie in the corner, buried in the couch.

"Great," Ty says, turning away. "That's all we need . . . a Blasting Cap baby."

"A little powder keg," Jay coos, rocking his arms back and forth.

I roll my eyes.

"A little six-shooter." Jay continues, his Vans keeping pace with me as I make my way toward Billie across the worn, dingy red carpet that is decorated exclusively with cigarette burns and strange wet spots.

After our first night sharing a bill, I know these things for certain: Blasting Cap likes alcoholic beverages, Billie, and blowing things up.

Their show is the Fourth of July and a mini Mardi Gras rolled into one, complete with smoke screens, small explosions, and a steel drum. By their third song the stage is knee deep in empty beer bottles and burned matches. Ty and I didn't stick around for the after-party last night, but Billie must have.

"Whatcha up to, Billie?" Jay asks, grinning down at her as we approach the battered couch. It has seen better days, probably ten years ago.

Billie stops to take a breath.

She swings her head up in our direction. Her eyes are lusty and unfocused, her cheeks shining pink.

"Sinning in the name of rock and roll," she says with a smile.

Jay chuckles.

"Well, stop," I say.

I reach down and peel her and the sweaty cap apart.

"It's time to cool down a little," I say. "And—"

Oh, crap, it isn't the cute one, I realize. It's the one with the teeth.

"Swab for diseases."

I yank Billie up by her wrist, steady her out, and straighten her skirt. She smells a little like gunpowder.

Holding her tight by the elbow, I steer her across the room.

As we turn the last dim corner and step onto the stage, she hisses into my ear. "I'm singing them all tonight." Her breath is smoky and sour.

Strange cylinders line the edge of the stage, every couple of feet. They must be new, compliments of Blasting Cap and their special effects team. His name is Dave.

"No, you're not." I assure her, and myself, as we navigate through the maze of old coffee cans and our gear.

"We'll see."

She twists away, bobbles on a loose cord, and finds her balance. She isn't that drunk tonight, but man, is she mean. I leave her alone, cranking her mic stand down inch by inch as I take my own spot onstage, on the audience's far right, and slide my guitar over my head.

Late last night when I was in bed, staring at the ceiling and waiting for the stars shining so brightly in my mind to fade so I could finally fall asleep, I thought about performing, about my music, about something that I created, that didn't exist until I thought of it, and I realized I will never want anything more than this. It is awesome and painful and sweet all at the same time. It fills me up and then craps me out the other side, ready for another go.

I smile to myself onstage, watching as my little sister brushes the hair out of her eyes and wipes the spit from some snaggle-toothed boy from the corners of her mouth.

Billie can make all the messes and sing all the cover songs she wants. Tonight it is finally my turn.

Our third song starts with a roll and a punch. Then the rush hits me. This is my song! A chorus of butterflies carrying chain saws circles in my stomach.

It's not like I didn't know it was coming. How many times did I hear Winston repeat our plan before the show: open with two covers, slide in a new song, and then get back to what they came here for? At least twice, but it felt more like ten.

But then Billie scratched over the set list with her boot, and I guess I really am lost in the sunshine of your love because I am totally surprised when Jay bounces down three bass notes of the intro, hard and heavy, announcing my song, my shot. Here it is.

The crowd swims before me, eyes and hair and teeth and smiling and clapping and waiting and watching and wanting, as I reach for the microphone.

Blood shoots through my veins, a thin, hot river of adrenaline. My mouth tastes tinny, like I licked a guitar string.

My heart rams at the walls of my chest, trying to escape. Please, ribs, I beg, don't break.

Billie steals one last look at me and goes off. She is a lit fuse, running and twirling and dancing. A hot flash of white legs and blond hair that streaks across the stage in a short black skirt while the rest of us race to keep up.

I open my mouth to sing and am slammed back by a sharp, deafening squeal of feedback. I cringe and cower away as a loud pop jolts the stage and everything is swallowed up by a deep, sudden darkness. Then silence.

It probably doesn't last more than a few seconds, but as I stand there on the stage with the microphone in my hand, that quiet feels like forever.

My mouth is open. The tips of my fingers are throbbing.

"Aww . . . Christ," Ty moans from behind me.

I hear his sticks land on top of his snare. "Blasting Cap blew out the lights."

Not just the stage lights, all the lights. And not just the lights, all the electricity, it seems. The only things still glowing are the exit signs above the doors and a Schlitz malt liquor lamp on the bar that looks so fossilized it probably runs on kerosene or melted whale blubber.

I swallow my disappointment in a large, disquieting gulp and cram the microphone back into its stand with sweaty fingers.

The crowd rustles self-consciously. I can feel fear and

excitement and confusion rising from the floor. A single shout goes up.

A generator kicks in, and the lights come on again, half-mast and ghostly green. A sigh and some clapping come from the mass of bodies below.

"Those sad little pyros," Winston swears as he walks on from backstage, lighting a cigarette and rolling up his sleeves.

"AFI wannabes." Jay joins in, reaching for a cigarette.

Winston bends down and tries one of the amps. Nothing.

Ty stands, slips his sticks into his back pocket, and walks over.

"We look like schmucks waiting around up here," he worries. "Like amateurs."

Jay laughs. "We are amateurs."

I unplug my guitar. Pull it over my head and set it on the floor as I search the stage. My heart thuds and stops.

"Where's Billie?" I ask.

A slippery curl of smoke is leaking from one of the coffee cans in the front corner, catching my eye. I cross the stage and find my sister there, down on the floor, standing with a small crowd circling her.

She is gray and crooked. Her arm is hanging funny, and I can see a line of sweat above her brow, even in the half-light of the generators.

I jump down off the edge of the stage.

"Billie?"

She is breathing hard, tears welling up in the corners of her eyes.

"Something's not right," she says.

Then she pukes all over me.

16

Billie rolls over and knocks into me with her cast. It is bright white in the early-morning light and scratchy. She drops it on the pillow next to my head. Her eyes flutter open, and she whimpers, "My prostaglandins hurt."

I try to move her fat white arm over without hurting her, but it won't budge, as if the plaster and the bedsheets have become one. I slide myself out of its way instead—sleeping beside Billie has always been a contact sport—and she falls back to sleep.

I reach over and touch the tips of her fingers, lightly. Last night an ER nurse in light blue scrubs wrapped Billie's skinny arm in plaster until it weighed more than Billie.

I watched, sitting on the edge of the hospital bed. I held Billie's free hand, the fingertips of her right hand on the verge of disappearing under all that wrapping.

"Dad, she's okay," Winston said from the other side of the thin white curtain that hung between us.

Two more wraps, and Billie's fingers would be gone.

"She's fine," he said. "Just a broken arm."

Just, I thought. Dad probably loved that: just a broken arm.

"No, you don't need to come. I can handle it."

I saw his boots pacing. They passed once, turned around, and kept going.

"We're all fine." His voice drifted down the hall that smelled like pain coated over with Pine-Sol and a little bit of prayer.

Shing! The nurse was done. She pulled the white curtain open, exposing Billie to the world again. My sister looked skinny, compared with that cast, and she smelled awful, like smoke and puke and plaster.

When Winston got us back to the capital H hotel, I crawled into bed with Billie, knowing I was going to be battered and abused, but certain that she shouldn't be alone. She already had a broken arm, one bruised rib, and three prescriptions to be filled. Good thing she wasn't that drunk or we could have added a rap sheet to that list.

Careful not to move Billie or her arm, I roll over and feel for the prescriptions on the nightstand. I get a whiff of myself when I move. I am still wearing my shirt from last night, the one covered in Billie's puke and dried tears and my nervous exhaust.

I click the TV on, set it on mute, and find some cartoons for Billie to wake up to. I slide out of bed and grab a shirt off the chair on my way to the bathroom. It is Billie's, so it is going to be way too tight and way too sparkly, but its lack of little chunks of pink french fries glued to the front appeals to me.

The bamboo-printed wallpaper in the hotel bathroom is peeling, and the bathtub is older than my dad. It feels like the towels have been around since before his birth, too. My skin hurts a little when I dry off after my shower.

I knock on the door to Winston's room with dripping wet hair and Billie's prescriptions in my back pocket. He has the cash, and he knows the way. Everybody else can sleep in.

The Barracuda Lounge paid us for last night, even though we didn't finish our set. I think they were worried about getting sued. The Blasting Cap boys chipped in, too, once they saw how they had broken Billie. Miniature bastards.

Winston opens the door and tugs on a hooded sweatshirt and his leather jacket. His hair is wet, too. I hold out the car keys to him.

The van coughs into life, and Winston pulls hard on his first cigarette of the day. I count the remaining cash, and he turns on the radio, flipping past NPR and morning talk until he finds some rock. His leg bounces all the way to the drugstore.

Winston doesn't like hospitals, doctors' offices, pharmacies, funeral parlors, or hair salons. Basically any place sterile and possibly antiseptic. Still, he stands next to me, tall and tight, as we wait for Billie's prescriptions to be filled. His eyes are locked on the shiny tiled floor, and it feels an awful lot like the time he had to take me to the drugstore to buy my very first box of tampons.

He stood the same way that day, stiff and awkward, planted in front of a wall of pink and blue and lavender boxes. He acted like we'd never met before while I searched the rows, looking for something familiar, a box I might have seen at school or under somebody's sink during a sleepover—but nothing.

I was nervous, standing there, trying to figure it out, just the two of us. My tears built, waiting for something to push them over the edge so they could spill down my hot, embarrassed cheeks.

Winston twitched his leg and reached for a royal blue box.

"These are the kind I think Mom used," he said, holding the box at arm's length, obviously out of his element.

They looked cheap. And generic. Nothing like anything that I would want to stick into my body. I shook my head no, my breath running at a rapid pace, and Winston put them back on the shelf.

Mrs. Cornwall, local school lunch lady and PTA president, was coming at us with a red store apron tied over her Christmas sweater and a tight smile on her face. Her rubber-soled shoes gripped onto the floor with a squeak and a squeak and a squeak.

I grabbed a soft pink box with the words "comfort glide" scrolled in the upper right corner before I heard one more squeak and started to cry right there in the tampon aisle. I headed for the cash register with my eyes down, wishing I had a mother.

Winston trailed behind me with a five-dollar bill in his hand, silent and steady, probably wishing the exact same thing.

A mother would be nice right now, too.

I wrap my jacket around me tighter, fighting off the onslaught of air conditioning. Like Winston said last night, it's just a broken arm. We will figure it out.

"Carter," the white coat behind the counter calls out.

"Carter," it repeats, louder.

I look over at Winston. He looks at me. We both look around. The place is overly fluorescent and completely deserted. There are only bottles of sweet cherry cough syrup, flushable undergarments, whiplash collars, and us. Why is this guy yelling?

We laugh and start to shuffle toward the counter to put the poor lab coat out of his misery.

"What will you do?" Winston asks.

"Is it only up to me?"

"Well," he says, "it is your band. Not mine. Or Billie's."

He looks over at me instead of staring at the floor.

"I don't know," I say.

Maybe this should be it. Maybe we should be done. Maybe

when your little sister twirls off the stage and snaps an arm, the universe is trying to tell you something.

I know that Winston wants to go on, that he has found some kind of honor in this, some code of the samurai, and he wants to do what he said he would and finish the tour. It is very un-Winston of him, and it makes me want to help him get there. But he isn't going to tell me what to do, not now, because then it will be his fault if it falls apart.

We step up to the counter.

"You could do it all, you know," Winston says as the lab guy pokes out our total on his computer screen. "Without her."

So he does want to keep going, broken arm or not, Billie or not.

"I know."

Winston pays with a smooth sheaf of bills pulled from his back pocket. I reach past him and grab the white paper bag.

He pauses. "But you won't."

The drugs knock and rattle inside the bag. No, I probably won't, I think as Winston curls the change in his palm and we walk toward the door.

And I hate that about me.

I flop back into bed as soon as Winston and I return from our early-morning run to the drugstore. I wake up hours later, all alone, with only an empty spot in the bed where Billie used to be. A pack of Sharpies lie open on her pillow. I lean up on my elbow and grab the closest one, stopping the pool of pink that is staining the sheets.

The TV, still playing silently, is now set to an infomercial for an exercise machine built of rubber bands. The room smells like brand-new markers and sleep.

I follow a trail of dirty clothes and find Billie in the bathtub, cast propped up on the edge, bubbles swirling around her body. All the towels are pulled off the metal rack and stacked on the floor at the edge of the tub, like bunting.

"How do you feel?" I ask, sliding down the wall next to the tub.

She points over the tip of her cast at the sink. Two of the orange pill bottles Winston and I picked up wait there, caps off. Pills litter the edge of the sink, melting in puddles and sticking to one another.

"Better."

She must have wandered out of the room while I was asleep; she already has scribbles all over her cast.

I reach for her arm.

"You've been busy," I say.

"Boom! Out Goes the Lights" is written in bright blue.

A random phone number is printed neatly in black near her elbow.

Dark green letters spell out "Way 2 Stage Dive! And "AWWWWwwww" is written in red ink, a long, twisting string that makes its way around the top edge of the cast and then trails down her wrist, getting smaller and smaller on its way back around toward her thumb.

Tugging her arm closer to me, I take the pink marker and write:

If Lost or Broken, Please Return to:

Teddy Lee

Tiny House at the End of the Street

Crazytown, USA

Billie reads what I've written, wrinkles her nose, and pulls her arm away. She points her toes and presses them up against the faucet.

"So . . . ," she says, slipping down, chin just above the water, "looks like my guitaring days are over. I should probably start learning your songs now."

Sighing, I press the back of my head hard against the wall. Of course that is what she thinks. I have something, and Billie wants it, no matter the cost.

I grab her before she can slide under.

"Not now," I say, wishing she were normal. Not broken and bruised and so damn Billie. I wish there were any way to win with her, any way other than giving in. "Not at least until your bone sets."

She splashes and looks away.

I push myself up from the floor, stop, and stare at myself in the mirror. I pretend not to see Billie in the background, picking at the fluff around the edge of her cast by her fingers, watching me, waiting for me to give in and change my mind like I always have.

Damn you, Winston, I think as I drop the marker and grab one of the sticky pills off the countertop. Why couldn't you be a ninja-level martial artist or a monster of motocross and just leave me alone? Leave me out of decisions and responsibility and the opportunity to disappoint everyone. Leave me to my music and myself, just like I was.

I wipe the pill dry with a hand towel from the floor, hearing a voice that is a lot like Winston's booming in the back of my head: " 'Cause nobody ever got famous playing the guitar alone in their bedroom."

Yeah? Well who says I want to be famous?

I don't stop until the rest of the pills are dry. I drop them back into the bottles, counting up the cost of each one as they plink into the plastic bottoms. I add them up, telling myself we can't afford to miss tonight. Not after a trip to the emergency room. There is no way I am going home with empty pockets, a dishonored brother, and a broken sister. The show must go on.

Billie turns on the tap with her foot. She toes it to the right, all the way past hot.

"Do you think you can do it tonight?" I ask, turning toward her and the mountain of steam rising from the tub.

She looks so tiny, so swallowed up. But she nods with

certainty. No big deal. No doubt.

I wish I knew what that feels like.

"Bring me some more bubbles," she says, just bossy enough to get the job done. "I'm starting to see the bottom."

So I pour them in, pink and pearly. They mix with the water, bubbling up to the edge, lapping at Billie's cast and broad grin. I add more, drowning her in a shimmering sea of hopeful sparkle, shine, and pop. Then I sink down, rest along the edge, and wait for her to wrinkle.

There is only a dusting of applause as our last notes drift over the stage and dissolve into the crowd. It lands on my shoulders and weighs me down.

Billie has been a pain in the ass all night. Tonight and every night of the week since she broke her arm, really, singing off-key and mumbling her way through the choruses, leaving me and the boys dragged down by the end of each set, wishing it were over.

But Billie won't be happy until she gets what she wants. No worries if that makes everyone else—especially me—hate her. She is used to getting her way no matter what, and since I am the only one who can give in and let her sing my songs, she's going to make every moment onstage miserable for me. Ty and Jay and Ginger are just along for the ride.

Ty's sticks tumble impatiently on top of his snare after we grind to a halt.

"Get your shitkickers out, boys!" Winston says sarcastically as he climbs up onto the stage from the dingy bar floor. "We might have to fight our way out tonight."

The crowd is milling around with straight faces and dirty work boots. Most of the drinkers sitting around the bar turned their backs on us during the last song, not even waiting until we got to the end to act unimpressed.

All the older men in plaid shirts and big belt buckles are making me miss my dad, miss home. It would be great to wake up and know where I am.

"Let's get the hell out of this bar." Ty pushes back from his drum kit with his eyes cast down and hooded, hiding from me.

"This is not a bar," Jay says. The flames on his guitar strap glimmer as the lights flash and then dim. "This is a sweat sock with a soda machine in the corner."

He's right. The bar is down a deep set of stairs, and it is cavernously dark inside. A shoebox with rectangular windows positioned way up high that glow with leftover streetlight. It looks like it used to be a bunker or a bomb shelter.

A small circular dance floor is cut out of dark carpeting. The barstools are black and fake leather, with high curved backs and long silver legs. They have those old glass candles, dark red and gold, wrapped in plastic netting sitting on the black horseshoe-shaped bar.

It is, I realize, the perfect place for our shit to fall apart. There was no opening band, no headliner, nobody to hide behind tonight. It was only the five of us, skimming along, trying to keep our heads up in this dark and dirty little bar. Things couldn't get much lower than this.

Winston crosses the stage, glowing red.

"Their money is still good," he says, grabbing the amp closest to him. I don't think he cares what we play, country or rock or funeral dirges, as long as we get paid.

Ty walks toward me, and I hold my breath, hoping he'll grab my hand and bring me back to center, whisper into my ear how everything will be okay and we'll find our way back somehow, but his eyes stay dark, studying the floor as he moves.

I follow him to the edge of the stage and wrap my fingers around his wrist. "Her arm won't be broken forever."

"No," he says, slipping free. "But for long enough."

His hands disappear, stuffed deep into his pockets. "Is this what you want for the rest of the summer? More nights like this?"

I know he doesn't want to give up on my songs, and neither do I. But I can't bring myself to hand them over. Not to Billie.

"It's great this way, Teddy Lee," he says, dropping down onto the first step, away from me. "You don't get to play your music. Billie doesn't get to sing your songs. And the rest of us don't get to play anything but covers. It's perfect."

He heads for the exit, leaving disappointment in his wake and my heart tightening up.

I should have just said no. No, Billie, you are never going to sing my songs. With no wiggle room. No chances. No gray area. But I didn't. I had to go and say something about her bone setting. I had to go and give her hope. And hope is a bitch.

I stomp over and snap the cord from my amp. The plug flies out and lands at Billie's feet.

"Just 'cause you're not happy," I say to her, "doesn't mean you have to suck."

"Why not?" she asks. "You do."

My fists clench, and my jaw squares as I eye her up. She does have another arm to break.

She drags her mic stand across the floor, pushes it into Winston's empty hands, and follows practically on Ty's heels, through the small crowd and up the dark stairs to the street.

Jay is standing off to the side of the stage, looking uncomfortable. He's holding his guitar against his hip at a strange angle. He bounces not at all.

Ginger is behind him in a shiny black shirt with silver cowboy detailing. It looks authentic, right down to the pearl buttons, but even that didn't help us tonight.

They start packing up their gear, quickly slamming cases and locking locks, all while stealing glances at me. They hop off the edge of the stage when they are done, one after the other, Jay like a gymnast and Ginger like a flamingo.

I wait while they climb the stairs, the light from the street slowly disappearing behind them as the door completely closes. It sucks knowing that standing up for myself is letting everyone else down.

Winston walks up beside me, winding a thick cord over his bent elbow and between his fingers.

"What do you think?" I ask him as he winds and winds and winds.

I am hoping I'm not the only one who thinks Billie shouldn't sing my songs. That someone else will vote in my favor—especially the guy who talked me into starting a band in the first place.

Winston knows what Billie is like.

He knows it won't be easy, but it might be worth it to try to keep something for myself. He has to see why I can't give in this time.

He is still. The bundled cord hangs slack in his hand.

"I think it's your band," he finally says, a single spot lighting up his shoe.

"You said that before."

"I know. Now act like it."

All I can hear is the scratch of silverware and the rustle of the newspaper next to me. Who reads the paper? I think, leaning away from the smear and ink of it until Ginger finally finds the rest of the story he is searching for, snaps the curling pages straight, and dives back in.

The morning sun is bright today, and my plate of steaming

eggs is yellow under a baby blue sky. I stare out the diner's front window with a ketchup bottle caught in my hand, struck by the fact that so much summer has passed us by.

It got lost in a bleary-eyed string of nightclubs and basement bars. I miss the smell of mowed grass, the sticky drip of a Popsicle melting down my fingers. I've seen so little of the sun.

I want to be awake at noon.

I want to know Ty in the daytime.

I miss the short shaved heads that started the summer. We are into August already and the boys are grown out now, completely shaggy and sullen.

Today we are heading west, turning back toward home. I don't want to think about that yet, though. The fact that real life is waiting for us, right around the corner. I try to tell myself we still have plenty of time.

Ty is going to Humboldt in the fall. That's the plan. He has semesters of hemp weaving and ethics seminars and a campus full of girls with thick, braided hair ahead of him. We have only a few more gigs to go. Soon summer will be over, and we all will be back home, breaking up, saying good-bye.

Ty has grown distant since Billie broke her arm, spending time alone, strumming his guitar or disappearing without a word. He is distracted now, always on to the next thing.

And Jay doesn't jump as high. He looks like his batteries are wearing out.

Ginger's fingers don't dance along to silent melodies anymore. His eyes don't light up as he scribbles notes and twirls his pencil, punctuating the air. His stillness speaks volumes.

We all need a vitamin.

I want everything back the way it was six weeks ago. Back when we were fresh and clean and new, covered in downy fuzz and anticipation. Before we wanted to bite one another's heads off.

Winston climbs into the booth, back from a smoke, and knocks Ginger's knees into mine under the table.

"I booked tomorrow night," he says, and then orders a Coke. Winston doesn't believe in coffee, only soda.

"It's big for us," he says, watching the waitress walk away. "Blasting Cap sent it our way. They were double booked."

Jay sniggers. "How is that possible?"

Winston shrugs. "People like smoke."

"Yeah," Jay says, "or ukulele-size guitars."

He pops up on the bench and starts playing his sternum like a guitar. Ginger watches over the top of his paper, his eyebrows up. Jay has one side of the booth entirely to himself. No surprise, since he is wearing his bright yellow I'm with Jealous T-shirt. It made Ginger and Winston and me all elect to cram in together on the other side.

Jay slides back into the booth when the waitress returns and bumps into the table on his way down. The table rocks. The water in our glasses shimmies.

"Anyway"—Winston continues after Jay settles down and Ginger's paper snaps back up—"it's gonna be loads of people, lots of cash."

That's good. After the last few nights it would be nice to have a shot at breaking even.

He twists the paper from his straw, tosses it aside, and takes a long dark drink.

"Who else?" I ask.

"A bunch of surf punks called Highway Robbery."

I nod. Time to get our shit back together then, because I plan on blowing them out of the water.

"Where are they now?" I ask.

Winston looks around, confused. "The surfing bandits?"

"No . . . Billie and Ty."

Winston shakes the ice around in his Coke.

"Maybe she's learning lefty," Jay says, strumming the air.

He stops, unhinges his jaw, and pours a glass of milk down his throat as I watch. One large white gulp and it is gone. Boys are such pigs.

Jay stifles a burp and adds, innocently, "It's not like she had that much righty."

True, but sometimes Jay is way too much like having another brother.

Winston sets down his Coke.

"So . . . you'll build a set list?" he asks, his long frame halfway out of the booth.

"Yep." I nod to his shoulder, his half-empty glass of Coke. I reach for my fork and stab some eggs.

Winston waves from the doorway, already pressing his phone against his ear as I start building the set list in my head.

It doesn't matter where Billie is right now—or Ty. I've decided I'm not giving in this time, no matter how broken any one of us might be. It is my band after all.

17

"*Scheisse …*"

Jay spins in a small circle, taking in the club.

It is big. Huge. As in seats-and-round-tables huge, room-down-front-for-dancing huge. Two bars. Even-has-a-balcony huge.

It must be an old-time theater that's been converted into a nightclub. White scrolled plasterwork edges along the ceiling and the balcony. The walls are covered in a plush dark red fabric, and the floor has a patterned carpet, intertwined vines that run the length of the room and twist together, dulled under years of spilled beer and foot traffic.

Winston finishes shaking hands with a dude in a navy blue sport coat who I am guessing must be the manager, then takes the steps leading up to the stage two at a time.

"Sweet, huh?" Winston asks us, a huge grin on his face.

We waited in a corner, letting him put on his responsible and mature managerial act while he got the full tour. He looks impressed.

"Let's load in, and then we have"—he grabs Ginger's wrist and checks his watch—"half an hour to sound check. So get your asses in gear."

"But first," he says before anyone can disappear. He reaches inside his jacket and pulls out five sheets of paper, rolled together into a makeshift tube. "The set list," he says, struggling to find the center of the pages.

We assemble in a loose circle around him while he smooths the papers flat against his chest. He hands one to each of us.

I take mine and prepare for Billie's perfect storm of bitching and moaning. It only takes a second.

"What is this shit?" she asks.

"They're called copies," Winston replies.

"This place has an office, too?" Jay looks up from scanning the page, still in wonderment.

Ginger and Ty stay silent, one on each side of me, papers down, far ahead of everyone else in reading comprehension.

"No." Billie's voice burns. "This shit." She taps the top of her copy with her fingertips. The cotton poking out the top of her cast is brown and dirty. She doesn't look at me.

Jay stops reading, finally catching on. His mouth gapes,

but he says nothing. He even stays still.

"Well, Bill," Winston says with a long breath, preparing for his explanation, "it's a big show, and we need to bring our best."

I cringe because that isn't the way we rehearsed it this morning when I handed Winston the set list. It was supposed to be something like "It's only one song, Billie, and you get all the rest and you are going to rock it." With a soft smile and maybe a candy necklace. He needs to baby her more. He knows that.

Billie drops her copy. The curled page drifts to the floor as her boots clomp, first to the right, aimlessly, and then change course, heading left toward backstage. She turns back at the doorway and glowers at me.

Jay and Ginger shuffle around and look at their feet.

"Get started without her," Winston announces. "I'll set up her stuff."

I hesitate, knowing this is not the end. Billie will not give up so easily.

Ty stands with his chin lifted, watching Billie go.

I desperately want to see him right now: his face, his eyes. I want him to look down at me the way he used to at the beginning of the summer, when he was so eager and I was so sure.

But he turns and brushes past me, knocking me off kilter.

All the time I've spent with Billie and her broken arm over

the past few weeks, I want to take it back with my lips, my fingers. I miss him.

I close my eyes and think of the first time I kissed him. How it felt, light and warm and tingly, my stomach dancing, not dripping with hot battery acid like it is now. I hold on tight for a few seconds, my lids blinking, and wait for Ty to return to me, to be the boy I used to know.

Winston grabs my arm, and my eyes pop open.

"You're sure about this?" he asks.

Ty drops into action on the far side of the stage, his muscles moving as he pulls gear across the floor with Jay without a word or a glance in my direction. As if he doesn't see me at all.

I nod and reach for my guitar. I think I am.

One by one the mass becomes a mob, and then the mob becomes a throng. Out front the club is coming alive. I can hear it filling up with the hum and chatter of people, the tink of stacking beer bottles, the clink and chunk of cash registers being stocked for the night.

Backstage our headliners are busy trashing their dressing room. They are going for legendary status. I shudder against the sound of splitting wood and creaking joints.

"Awww, come on!" Jay groans from behind me.

His complaint is followed by laughter from Highway Robbery.

"We're too poor to smash guitars!" he adds, and they laugh louder.

A double bill with Highway Robbery and Blasting Cap must be a path of destruction. I hope we won't disappoint. The only thing that gets smashed at our shows is Billie.

Highway Robbery started early, sacking their dressing room as soon as we finished our sound check. They called it a preparty, and two hours later the plaid couch and the keg of beer in the corner are the only items that remain intact.

When the TV drops to the floor for the second time, I wiggle off my broken barstool and leave Winston, Jay, and Ginger in the rubble. Ty slipped away down the slim hallway long ago, avoiding the party like always.

I feel boyish eyes on me all the way to the door, mannish ones, too, so I am careful not to move so fast that my ass shakes. I turn into the hall, taking tiny geisha steps in my tall black boots. I'll save the staring for when I am onstage, thank you very much.

Stopping backstage, I steal a look through the curtains at the swell of the crowd.

The lights are dim, but from back here I can just make out the bartenders pulling taps and pouring beers as fast as they can under a chasing string of colored lights. They finish the beers off with a splash and a perfect streak of foam at the top as the lights speed back to the other end of the bar and then start again.

This is, by far, our biggest audience yet. Girls and guys and some that look like both are working it in worn leather and ripped denim, everyone smoking and texting and looking for somebody to take home at the end of the night.

They are a boiling thundercloud of energy and anticipation that bounces against the stage. Their expectations hover overhead, reaching down like fingers that stretch out and feel for me, trying to find me and figure me out.

I skirt around the back edge of the stage and head for the safety and quiet of our tiny dressing room, picturing only the set ahead and the list of songs that hold it together.

RED VELVET CRUSH is printed in some PC font on a plain sheet of white copy paper and taped to the door. I reach for the knob and turn it.

The door won't budge. It isn't locked, but stuck. Wedged.

I smell the sweet shadow of pot smoke. Billie laughs on the other side of the door. I push hard against the cracked wood, putting some shoulder into it. The door gives, and I trip over the threshold.

It is chilly in the hall, the air conditioning blasting, but the room is muggy and smells of smoke and sweat. The lights are off, and my eyes have to adjust to the darkness.

Ty's head turns. His eyes are glazed, his brain elsewhere. His sticks poke out of Billie's back pocket. I grip on to the doorknob.

I don't see everything at first. Only bits and pieces. Blink.

Horror. Blink. Hurt. Blink. Heartbreak.

I stand, trying to take it in.

The bottles. The rolling papers. Billie's hand on his knee, the worn, dirty bottom of her boots as she kneels down in front of him, so comfortable, so close. Her face as she twists toward the door, long blond curls spilling over her shoulder. Her smile when she sees me.

My heart races and explodes.

It is the big finish, the final end to our great rock 'n' roll song. The drums crash, the bass thrums. Blistered fingertips blaze along a wire-hot guitar string, and I stand, frozen with my toes at the edge of the stage and watch as my life falls apart.

I bash into Ginger in the hallway but stumble on, my fingertips sliding down an endless wall. The floor leans and tilts, coming up to meet me, then pulling away. I flinch against the hanging bare bulbs and the sound of smashing guitars.

I push into the bathroom. Lock myself in a stall, breathing, heaving. I am shaking like tremolo, with puky spit and shaky hands.

The bitter bile of betrayal rises in my throat, choking out my breath, burning my eyes with tears, and sticking my hair to the back of my neck.

My mind is flying, faster than fingers on a keyboard doing scales, chasing, racing, looping to come back and bite me again, tearing this time with teeth that drip with blood.

I am such a fool. An idiot.

I gulp in the stall air. Curl my hands into fists and pound into the wall. GO AHEAD AND SIT DOWN, someone scribbled on it. CRABS CAN JUMP FIVE FEET.

Toes appear on the other side of the stall. Worn boots I know too well. I can see the bulge of her baby toe rubbing through on the right side.

My mind is filled with hatred and anger, but in a moment of surprising clarity, I realize she is going to need new shoes soon.

"Nothing happened," she says.

She sounds so close. Like she is pressed up against the stall door. I stagger and sit down, not even worried about the crabs.

"I didn't do anything."

Of course she'd say that. She says that about everything. The world just happens around her. Disasters abound, and Billie is blameless, innocent and doe-eyed, sitting in the middle of my catastrophe.

She comes closer to the door. I shift, sliding away. Sorry, Billie, but there's no coming back from this one.

She has taken everything—my music, my heart, even my faith in her—and left me with nothing but a mouthful of shit. I can taste it curling down my throat and settling to rot against my teeth.

I don't care anymore. Billie can have it all. She can sing everything.

There is nothing left for me now. Here is the end, and holy shit, does it hurt.

The bar is thumping loud, a cinder-block millstone behind me as I stand in the middle of the dark parking lot with nothing to my name but an old cardigan with a patched elbow.

I step into the streetlight and look down the street. Which way did we come from? Where is the hotel? How the hell can I get away from here, and how long will it take? I feel like I've spent the last six weeks living with my eyes closed.

I've had nightmares like this, I think.

Winston comes swinging out of the back door of the bar in a blast of music. Ginger is right behind him. They are moving fast. I hate that they know what happened. That everyone knows.

I shrink back, out of the light. If Ty comes through that door, I am going to lose it. I am already a snotty, puffy mess. My throat hurts.

Winston grabs my arm and hustles me toward the van. I cross my arms and let him walk me along. The van is right there, parked right in front of me all along.

"Take her back to the hotel," he says, lighting a cigarette in the middle of it all. He tosses the car keys to Ginger. "I'll go inside and figure this out."

Ginger opens my door and trots around to his side to start the van.

"Come back for us later," Winston shouts. "When she's okay."

It takes me two tries to pull myself up into the passenger seat. My boot keeps slipping, and my arms feel weak. Like I am ever going to be okay again.

The engine is cold, and the van roars and squeals as we back up and drive down the street, away from the bar. I slip down into my seat and stare at the passing streetlights, so glad for once that Ginger doesn't have a single word to say.

Somewhere in the middle of the night a phone rings. I'm not really sleeping. I'm not really awake. I am barely there. My eyes have been staring blindly as the sky dips from battered blue down to deep purple and then slowly descends into pure, deep night.

I reach for my phone, but it's the one beside the bed.

"It's Ben," the other voice says, "from Blasting Cap."

Even in the dark I can see his fingers shooting an imaginary gun.

I wait.

"Billie's here with us."

Of course she wouldn't stick around to face up to what she'd done. At least I didn't need to picture her ending up all alone in a gutter somewhere, with cracked lips and imaginary bug holes scratched into her face.

"She didn't want me to call, but I found the number

anyway. I thought you should know."

He pauses.

"I'd want to know if Billie was mine," he says as if she were a purse or a lost sweater. "We're finally on our way to Seattle. She says she wants to come along."

I rest my head down. The phone is so heavy in my hand. I breathe out and he keeps going.

"I guess Glen gave her his number."

I see black numbers on a white cast.

"Let me give it to you."

The number bounces around inside my head, and I roll over. Don't bother, I think. You can keep her.

"I hear heartbreak makes for great music, Teddy Lee."

I drop the phone onto the desk. That's good to know. Then I am a goddamn gold mine. The phone lands, knocking over some empty pill bottles and a bunch of Billie's other crap.

I long for a way to wipe out what happened tonight and everything else from the last five months. My arm scrapes across the desk, dumping everything onto the floor as my jaw starts to shake.

Billie's bag sticks out from under a chair. I grab it and cram in everything I can find: undies, jeans, her toothbrush, curled magazines, mismatched shoes, shirts, even her mostly used soap from the shower.

A sleeve still pokes out when I zip the bag shut and check

the room. It is good enough. I wipe my eyes, take the chain off the door, and dump it all in the open hallway in a heap. For once someone else is going to have to clean up Billie's mess.

A car is in the lot out front, waiting with its parking lights on. The engine is running, a soft humming that climbs its way up to the second floor.

"Thanks for calling, Jay." A familiar voice sneaks up the open stairway and across the all-season carpet. I stop, hiding myself in the safety of my doorframe. "I know it was hard."

Ty's dad.

I creep out of the shadows and tiptoe toward the voice. Four people are moving in a slow shuffle across the parking lot. Jay and Ty's dad are walking in front. Jay has his hands jammed in his pockets. Ty's dad carries his duffel.

Ty follows with his mom. He walks slowly, curved over, his head down. His dad opens the car door, and Ty ducks into the backseat, like an outlaw. His mom climbs into the passenger seat, and Jay bends down toward Ty, his checkered Vans rocking to the sides. He leans in, talking quietly. I can't hear a word.

Jay finally stands. He pushes the door shut, quiet in the night. Ty is shrouded and invisible behind tempered glass.

His hand resting along the top of the car, Jay thumps twice—drive safe—and they take off. There is a flash of bright headlights, the whir of new tires gripping wet pavement, and that is it. Ty is gone. The sun hasn't even thought about cracking the sky, spilling orange and purple and liquid all over a new day.

I buckle and back into the room. The door shuts slowly behind me, my heart imploding into a billion pieces with the click of the latch, until I am only bits and pieces, a disappearing star, floating in a black, black sky.

just me and the sky

18

Dad is waiting up for us when Winston and I get home. Winston called ahead, telling him about Billie and about me. Dad is ready—arms out. He wraps me up in a hug as soon as I walk in. Winston leans against the counter and watches my bags drop to the floor.

I might hold on too long, maybe squeeze too tight, but in the dusky hours of early morning, my dad rocks with me and doesn't let go. All my music is gone, I want to tell him; I only hear the flat, empty sound of space.

We drove forever and ever to get home. The boys took turns at the wheel, stoic and solitary, while I sat in the back, curled up on the bench. I couldn't talk. I didn't know what to say. I wanted to be anywhere else, anybody else. I don't even know what really happened, only that I was there and Billie was not. And neither was Ty.

In the end there wasn't much to decide or much to do. Two of our band members had disappeared. We had only three shows left anyway.

Winston spent the day canceling and apologizing and talking to Randy. Jay and Ginger holed up in their room, probably watching Mexican soap operas or composing intricate power ballads.

I stayed alone, sitting and crying, lying down and crying. Wiping my eyes with cheap hotel Kleenex until my skin screamed, looking out the window, longing for home. I checked my phone, blinking against its glare in the darkened room. No texts. No messages. I missed Ty.

Then I swore for a while. Punched the bed. I think I even slept.

Late in the day Winston banged on the door. "Let's go."

My eyes swept the room. The worst night of my life happened here, I thought. Flowered bedspreads will always make me sad.

There was little left of Billie. An earring I stepped on in the night. A sock. Some hair spray. And one empty orange pill bottle, same as those in the dressing room the night before, glowing bright and clacking together on the table next to Billie and Ty.

I picked it up and read the label: AS NEEDED FOR PAIN. I dropped it onto the unmade bed. Looks like they worked; I have never hurt so much.

With each mile closer to home I gradually started coming back into focus. There's our exit . . . our town . . . our corner . . . our streetlight . . . our mailbox. Next stop, lonesome town.

Now I am afraid I am going to be cold forever—cold and wet and lonely. Stuck in this quiet, empty place in my brain, feeling these feelings. A storm cloud has settled in over my life, and I'm scared there will never be a wind strong enough to blow it away.

I avoid my bedroom at first and head for the bath instead. I can't look at myself in the mirror, so I swing the medicine cabinet open while I turn on the tap.

Our water heater takes a while to do hot. It's better now, but when we were little, lukewarm was all we had. I remember my dad describing the water that way, and it sounded so good to me. I immediately wanted a boyfriend named Luke Warm. He would have big hands and brown eyes, with soft, smooth skin that was satiny on my cheek when we kissed.

I love you, Luke Warm. I shivered, waiting next to a naked little Billie for the tub to fill.

Steam fills the tiny bathroom and fogs up the window and any chance at my reflection. I shut the cabinet door and sink in, my hollow bones filling with hot water.

I hover over the water, arms stick straight on the sides of the tub. I'm unable to let go and let the heat pull me in and soften me up. I'm afraid of what will follow: the tears, the remembering. The aftermath.

The grainy stop-action film that has filled my thoughts since last night starts to play again. It's been skipping through my head, frame by frame, over and over, every hour, every minute, every moment—long and stretched out and interminable. I shake my head. Worst movie ever.

Music trails in to take its place as I sink into the tub; a haunting whisper of guitar overtakes the gurgle of water. I let my eyes shut and drift, but it isn't a dream. I hear a chord, two notes, and another chord. I breathe them in as they steal in under the bathroom door, steady, true, and real.

I pull the plug with my toe and stand up in the steamy air. My hair drips down my back, and I hope to see my pain swirling down the drain, a trail of lather and heft that circles clockwise and then disappears. But I don't. It is too deep inside, hidden away where soap and bubbles and a soft towel can't get to it.

I dry off and follow the notes down the hall. Dad is sitting at the kitchen table, lit only by the blue flame hissing under the kettle. His toes rest one on top of the other, clean white socks with red stitching along the toe. A guitar sits in his lap and a coffee mug at his elbow.

My eyes trace his fingers. My own fingers flex, reaching out for strings that aren't there. I reach up and rub my neck where my strap always sits. My skin soaks in his melody, and I am filled with a sharp, deep emptiness.

"Sorry," Dad says when he realizes I am there, leaning

against the wall in the dark hallway. He silences the strings with the flat of his hand. I shake my head softly, not wanting him to stop.

"It's good," I say as I move toward him.

"And you?" he asks before he looks down.

He finds his fingering and starts again.

I don't know if he means my music or me, but the answer is the same: shattered.

"He could have been everything," I say.

I take a breath. It is so hard to miss someone and hate them at the same time. And right now I hate and miss Ty and Billie in equal measure.

Dad's rough fingers slide along a string as he straightens himself up to look at me. He seems more solid, more sure of himself than before we left.

That makes me a little jealous. Not that I want his life to suck, but it feels like he found himself in solitude, while I went off on a great and horrible adventure only to come home more broken and lost.

"Nobody else should be everything," he says, leaving a shivering note floating between us. "Then where are you?"

Right here, standing in my pajamas in the dark, the loser who gave everything away to my soul-sucking little sister and the best boy I ever met when I should have kept something for myself. I swallow that down, trying to find a place for it to sit in my stomach as I turn away.

Dad keeps strumming, winding his way through a familiar tune that waltzes me into my bedroom.

I steel myself in the doorway before I walk inside. Billie is everywhere: on the bed, tumbling out of the closet, dancing across the floor. Even the air inside still smells like her perfume.

I pause on the pink rug and wonder: Which is worse, never knowing your sister or knowing your sister and wishing that you didn't?

Right now I vote for the never knowing, because the other one is making me remember everything—every embarrassment, every triumph, every betrayal, and every sunshiney moment. They claw at my heart and squeeze the tears from my eyes.

I shut the door, launch my backpack onto Billie's bed, and watch her stuffed animals bounce.

A kitten drops to the floor as I climb under my covers.

There's a plane outside my window, blinking on and off as it steals across the night sky. It pulses, a singular heartbeat at fifteen thousand feet, pacing me as I curl up and wait for the stars to settle, for this day to be done, for the empty silence inside my head to finally stop.

The sun is bright this morning, way too bright for someone not even two weeks into total heartbreak. The house is too quiet, too. And someone is knocking on the front door.

I roll over. Go away. Get off my porch.

They knock again.

Please stop knocking, please go away, and please die—in that order. I put my pillow over my head.

Another loud knock tells me Dad and Winston must be gone. One of them would have stormed to the door by now. I sit up and rub my eyes, feeling sick and groggy from sleeping so late. Sleeping is good, though. It stops the silence.

Knockety knock knock knock. Knock.

Oh my God. I huff out of bed, wrench my bedroom door open, and head for the front door.

Jay is on the other side, his arms straddling the doorframe, his freshly shaved head poking right in at me. Stunned, I smile before I can stop myself. Then I look behind him for Ty. Old habits die hard.

"So Winston thinks he's keeping the van?" he asks, thumbing toward the front yard, where the van is parked as he walks through the open door.

"Looks that way," I say.

I follow him across the living room and sit down cross-legged on the couch. I got crushed, and Winston got the van. He probably thinks we came out even.

Jay is wearing dark jeans and a white T-shirt with a surfer on it that says "Can't we all just get a longboard?" He takes over the lounger, flipping the footrest up and leaning back.

I try to smooth down my hair when he's not looking,

wondering why I care; he's seen me in worse shape.

"I came to say good-bye," Jay announces, sounding awfully grown up.

Even in my state of disrepair, I am pleased. Not a lot of people take the time to say good-bye to me. They usually just disappear.

"Off to school," I say, very aware that Ty would have been off to college now, too, right along with Jay. That no matter what happened, we would have been saying good-bye.

He could still be going, I guess, but I'm not thinking about that.

"Yep"—Jay sighs—"off to school."

I can see Jay in a decked-out dorm room full of speakers and kick-ass stereo equipment and a remote control for everything. He will wire it all up to the light switch and blow the university's circuits on the first day.

He crosses his arms behind his head, squeaking on the worn leather chair.

Next week my senior year starts. Billie should be a sophomore, but it looks like she isn't coming back.

We should have known that she would turn out to be just like my mom. All the signs were there: the slutty-chic fashion sense, the accidental cigarette burns, the utter disregard for schedules and personal boundaries, and now the ability to abandon everything at a moment's notice.

"Maybe someday we'll get the band back together," Jay

says, staring at a stack of *Auto Traders* that Winston left on the end table.

Here it comes, I think, the thing that breaks your heart.

"Ty would like it," he says, glancing at me.

That line is a torpedo to my stomach. Ooof. The sun does a deep dive inside me.

Jay folds the leather chair down in a sudden, swift movement. He squeezes tight onto the armrests and then breathes out, one big, long breath.

"About him and Billie . . ." he says.

So, this is why he is here. I can't make myself look up at him. I study his hands instead. His nails are short and clean. He really is all ready for school.

"They did some things they shouldn't have."

My head starts to swim. I can still smell the pot smoke; see the glaze in Ty's eyes. The sight of the bottom of Billie's boots is burned into my brain.

"They were hanging out," he says.

Yep. And hooking up—the fact that Ty fell for Billie's shit, that he went from not noticing her at all in the beginning to jumping right into the trap she had set for him—that hurts most of all. He's a smart boy with a fancy high school diploma. He should have seen her coming. So should I.

Jay leans forward and taps my knee.

"Teddy Lee, they got drunk; they got high. But that was it. That was all."

Was it?

Jay is watching me with raised eyebrows. Maybe that's what he heard, but I know Billie better than that. Don't I?

Slowly I sink back into the couch and stare straight ahead, the shattered bits of what I thought had happened rearranging in my mind. I remember all the times Ty disappeared on his own, his silence toward the end of the trip. I thought Billie was the one getting high that night, not him.

Did she push Ty over the edge or did he run and jump?

Does it even matter? I only saw him crash.

Maybe if I had stayed with Ty every night or if I had given in like I always did and let Billie sing my songs, she would still be here, Ty would still be mine. Maybe I could have saved us all somehow.

I'm overcome with the sudden desire to smoke, the need to have something to do with my fingers, an excuse to look busy and do something self-destructive at the same time.

"He didn't ask me to come." Jay wipes his palms along the front of his jeans. "I haven't seen him since that night. No visitors and all that."

He rests his freshly tanned arms on his knees and says to me, earnestly, "I thought you should know. I thought it might help."

I feel like I should say thanks, but I'm not sure I want to. There has to be more to the story, but I might only ever get to know half of it. And I have to find a way to live with that.

The leather chair rocks and squeaks as Jay gets up. He stands in the middle of the living room, waiting for me. I know he's trying to make things right, but that doesn't make them hurt any less.

I stand up and step toward him. He squeezes me tight, a good hugger, lifting me off my toes.

"It was the best band ever," he says over my shoulder.

I try to laugh a little, but it is just air in the shape of a smile.

"Way better than the Trigger Brothers," he says as he sets me down.

My toes touch the floor, and I let him go.

"It made the Trigger Brothers seem like a popgun," he adds, stopping at the front door to shoot his fingers at me, Ben style.

I watch him through the front window as he walks out across our grass and past the whitewashed van.

He turns back when he gets to his car and waves with a hopeful smile and a big Jay bounce that breaks my heart all over again because he is back to normal and I don't even know where to begin.

19

Being a senior gets me a better locker, but that's about all I can say to recommend the experience so far. Everyone is running around, crazed and college bound, talking about scholarships and grants and early acceptance.

College is not even on my mind. All those decisions still seem light-years away somehow, completely insignificant, even though I am here every day, books and backpack, pens and paper in hand.

I am glad to be upright. Out of the house. Away from Winston's jiggling and Dad's worried looks. The farthest I can see down the road right now is the bell at the end of the day.

I thought about not going back. It seriously crossed my mind. And then I thought: How many hours a day can I spend watching stolen cable? Or swallowing down Winston's secondhand smoke? Sure, school kind of sucks, but at least they give me a ticket every morning for a free hot lunch.

Rumors about Billie flourish and grow. She is touring the world. Has leukemia. Got knocked up over the summer and was sent away to a home for wayward girls to save our family from further embarrassment.

On the fourth day of classes, one of the rumors catches up to me in the library during study hall. My books are spread out in front of me on a round table, warding off any spirited sophomore with bad skin who might decide to sit down next to me sporting his first boner. It happens.

Instead I get two little freshman girls in striped tights, short skirts, and tiny T-shirts stretched over long john tops. Billies in training.

The one with auburn hair steps up to me and says, "Is it true your sister ran away with a carny?"

The other one gulps.

I look up from my notebook and stare.

"Yes," I say. "She did."

The two freshmen turn and look at each other wide eyed.

I sit up straight and glance around the room before I lean in closer.

"I saw them," I say. I slide my American literature book over and nudge her beige little fingernails off my table. "They all had tiny hands."

She pulls her hand back and grabs her friend by the arm,

their chain-linked purses swinging as they skitter across the quiet library, only checking back once to glare at me.

At least that version of the story is closest to true: the Blasting Cap boys are freakishly small. But mostly I let people believe whatever they want. September is slipping by one week at a time, and I am still rocking myself to sleep at night, watching the moon make its way across my window. The world is still moving; life, apparently, still goes on. My heart doesn't believe it much.

I sleep little, and my dreams are full of long, empty hallways and glimpses of Ty—his back, his arm, his hand—but never him.

Billie shows up, too, in somebody else's shoes, smiling like the Cheshire cat. I miss seeing her messy blond hair pooling on top of her pillow across the room in the moonlight. I even miss hearing her annoying loud breathing when I wake up.

I stay in my bed late one Saturday morning, feeling battered and frayed, another week's worth of schoolwork and just as many sleepless nights behind me. My fingers are stiff. I haven't played in so long.

My nose is cold outside the blankets. It is finally, definitely fall. The weak slant of light sneaking under my curtains confirms it. Fall.

I roll over, smushing my pillow so it will fit my neck, and listen to Dad outside my door as he packs his lunch in the kitchen and leaves.

Rolling onto my other side, I wait for Winston.

He coughs to life. There is the flick of a lighter, the flush of the toilet, and then the slam of the front door. The van roars from the front yard before it calms down and then rattles away down the street. Will Jay ever come back and take that thing away?

Flipping over again, I face the wall, snuggling down under my quilt and the extra blankets I stole from Billie's bed. I stretch, slipping into the soft sheets and silence of the empty house, reminding myself that swimming around in thoughts and memories of Ty won't do me any good. He is still gone. So is Billie.

I think I hear something in the garage. It sounds like a guitar. I lie still, my ears straining. Thieves don't usually tune up before stealing your shit, do they?

There's the creak of the side door and the sound of shifting, as if the boxes and other crap out there were being put into place. Followed by a bass line—I'm pretty sure. The windows shimmy in their frames.

I sit straight up. Is that "Smoke on the Water"?

I tiptoe out of bed and peek out the corner of my window. The side door to the garage is cracked open. The glass in front of me vibrates with a low, long note. I grab a sweatshirt, pull it on over my pajamas, and head for the garage.

The grass between the house and the garage was a beaten-down dirt path when we left, but over the summer, it had a chance to sprout up and spread out.

My bare feet step lightly on top of the springy green shoots, and I pass the peony bush, unsure what I am about to find, other than someone now playing The Doors, and playing them well.

I cross the threshold to the garage with the doorknob held tight in my hand. My guitar has been set up across the room. It rests against a stool, the case locked and stowed under Winston's workbench.

Someone has straightened up since the last time I was in here. That was the night we got back, when all I could manage to do was dump my stuff into a shitty pile. Now I can see the floor; a semicircle has been swept clean. A road map of black cords navigates toward the nearest outlet.

Ginger Baker is standing in the shadows. He lifts his chin at me when I walk in, but he doesn't stop playing. I smile. It is the closest we have ever gotten to hello.

Blocks of morning light are breaking through the dirty windows of the garage door: warm, glowing squares that land on the spots where Billie and I used to stand. The sound of Ginger's guitar pulls me closer. When he can play like that, there is no need for us to talk.

I take a seat on a stool as Ginger rolls into another song. I listen, my toes curling around the base of the stool and warming in the morning sun.

The music loosens the lock on my thoughts, softening up the black hole that Ty left behind and towing me back to earth. I haven't played a note or heard a song in my head since the night I saw the two of them together. I didn't realize how much I have been missing it, how much it means to me. But I'm not ready yet. I just listen for now.

The squares of light grow warmer and brighter, song after song, as they slowly slide up the wall behind me while Ginger plays.

They are long and skinny and angled, stretching all the way up to the cobwebby rafters to shimmer there in the dust when he finally packs up his bag hours later and sneaks out through the crack in the side door, leaving his guitar resting next to mine.

Ginger shows up again on Wednesday after school. Dad and I are washing dishes when he suddenly appears, tall and skinny, rolling through the backyard on his gold twelve-speed.

He ducks under the clothesline with a soft guitar case strapped to his back and a plaid thermos gripped against his handlebars.

Dad looks over at me, and I shrug.

Winston leaves the table and squeezes in next to me to see through the window over the sink.

"He's baaa-aaaack," Winston sings quietly over my shoulder as we all watch Ginger lean his bike up against the side of the garage and walk into the open side door, taking the guitar off his back as he goes.

"Maybe he's in love with you," Winston says, grabbing a Coke from the fridge while I dry my hands on the dish towel.

"Maybe he misses his friends," Dad says, still staring out the window at the garage.

Maybe he's right. Ginger is a senior, like me. I have to remind myself that with Jay off at college and Ty gone, his friends have disappeared, too.

"I'm not convinced." Winston coughs, the soda bubbles biting at his lips and bursting into a misty spray as he gets ready to sip. "I'm picturing redheaded babies."

I toss the dish towel at him. To Winston, everything is a horny love story.

He laughs as I pull the kitchen door open and leave him grinning stupidly, catching the dish towel between his fingers without spilling a drop of soda.

Ginger brought an acoustic bass in the case on his back. He is tuning it as I walk into the garage. He has my guitar set up next to the stool again and a cup of coffee poured from his thermos waiting for him on the nearest amp. The air smells like axle grease and coffee beans.

This time I am ready. I slide onto the stool and set my guitar on my knee, the moon and stars strap swinging loose. I find my spot, the starting place my fingers call home. Ginger plays, leading me in. There is nothing else to do but close my eyes, feel the pop of each string, and focus. I am slow at first, but I lighten up.

Ginger is just as good on the bass as Jay, even if he doesn't jump around as much. Not that anyone could.

He pushes me, getting technical. Trying out songs that were never on our set lists, seeing where I can go. I do my best, feeling a little lost in my own skin, struggling sometimes to keep up. But he is patient and kind, if demanding.

Late in the day he sets his bass on the floor. He reaches for my guitar, lengthens the moon and stars strap, and then he plays for me, flat out, just him, and it is so good, so, God . . . orchestral, full of soaring notes and plummeting changes. He takes all kinds of melodies, historical and classic, and he turns and twists them, making them into a rock and roll song, showing me how it's done. That is our conversation.

When he leaves, an orange flash in the dark night, he leaves a book behind on Winston's workbench. I pick it up.

Music Theory, it says. It looks used but well loved. Two of the pages are marked with Post-Its and extremely sharp hand-drawn arrows. I grin, opening to the first one.

I am folding laundry on the couch when Ginger shows up with an electric keyboard on Thursday. Then, a couple days later, while I am putting away the groceries, he rolls in with a snare, followed by a high hat.

I half expect him to ride up the next Saturday morning fitted out as a one-man band, with a bass drum strapped to his back and a harmonica on a harp rack next to his mouth.

We take back the garage, pushing all of Winston's stuff to the side. Ginger rigs up a deal where he can play his guitar and the bass drum at the same time while sitting on the stool stolen from the auto parts store.

Winston watches sometimes, shoulder against the peeling doorframe, a halo of smoke over his head. I think he harbors hopes and dreams of loading up the van and hitting the road again.

What neither one of them knows is a few Mondays ago, the Monday after Ginger showed up for the first time, actually, I stood in line outside the band room with the misfits and their musical instruments and mixed orthodontia to meet my adviser for the first time.

It was first thing in the morning, and I was packed in next to a tuba player and some tiny kid with a saxophone so huge it could double as a foghorn.

I waited for my turn, resting against the cold brick wall, shifting and sliding my bag back up onto my shoulder. I spent my wait considering the cosmic irony that I had just now, after more than three years of high school, discovered that my adviser is also the music teacher. Maybe I should have visited sooner.

The office door finally swung open, and I slipped past a large girl with a tiny flute, cutting the tuba guy off at the pass. He smiled anyway.

"I want to change my schedule," I said to the comb-over sitting behind the desk, holding the necessary pink paperwork out in front of me.

"Why?" he asked without looking up.

"I want to sign up for individual study."

He stuck his arm out for my form.

"And what will you be giving up for such an honor"—he paused and read the first line—"Miss Carter?"

"Study hall."

"Concentration?" he asked.

"Music."

He finally looked up at me, his pen poised over the signature line of the form. Now I had his attention.

While everybody else is getting ready to go to college, I am going to get ready to go somewhere. It might not be college. It might just be the next town big enough to have a good music scene. And I will strum my fingers off to get there if I have to. I promised my dad at the beginning of summer that I would come back. I never said I would stay.

My long-lost adviser signed my form but never took his eyes off my mouth. "You look like you would have good embouchure."

Great, my adviser is a total perv. If there were any other way to get some time in the private music rooms without him, I would have walked out right then and there.

I snatched the paper away from him and turned to let the

tuba player in, hoping that at the very least, he had a leaky spit valve that needed to be fixed.

Now during third period of each and every school day, I sign in with the perv at his desk and listen to his instructions. Then I lock myself away in a tiny practice room with a fingerprinted black upright and a window the size of a business envelope, strumming and learning, skipping the assignment I have been given and making my way through Ginger's annotated book, one step at a time.

The solitude of the carpeted walls and the measured tick of the metronome loosen me up. It is a place that reminds me of nothing and nobody. The sun doesn't shine in, haunting me with spirits and specters and the whispers of soft kisses.

I unwind, testing my strength. There are no crowds, no encores, and no cover charges. Nobody twirls off the edge of the stage to barf or break a bone. It is completely mine.

And every day, without fail, Ginger rolls through my yard. I imagine him flying, long legs tripping toward my house, his head filled with strings and horns and odd three-quarter tempos.

He is technical and tight. He eats the cheeseburgers that Winston delivers to us in concentric circles, chomping smaller and smaller, spiraling until all that is left is the bite in the middle, the one with the pickle hidden under the bun.

He gets lost inside himself when the music goes dark and

moody, his eyes shifting to the floor, his shoulders leaning in toward each other, sinking his button-down shirts deep between his collarbones.

I always leave the book for him on the workbench as soon as I get home, open to the page that I got to or the step I got stuck on, and he will start with something from that page, a tricky tempo or time signature when I walk in, my hair still wet from the shower or my mouth dusted with cookie crumbs straight after school.

He tilts his head, listening to what I have been working on. Then he leads me in, backing me up, filling in the rough spots and dropped notes so that we can get past the theory and move on to my music.

We have little disagreements, moments when we try to outplay each other, but I find out fast that it is hard to argue with a boy who doesn't talk. His silence and his skill win out every time.

He always marks a new page or a new passage in his music theory book before he lights out the door.

We play for days and hours and evenings, sometimes until it is dark and in the morning sometimes, too, but mostly after school, while the ginkgo leaves turn and drop, leaving a yellow trail for Ginger's bike tires to follow as they tick, tick, tick down the wet drive on his way home.

We play while the sun sets with an orange sizzle behind the house, over and over and over, while the cold starts creeping in through the cracks of the garage in a major way and the air around our fingertips grows bitter and sharp.

We keep it loose and raw and a little unrefined until everything doesn't hurt as much. We play until I can hear the words and sing the songs and see myself in them again.

20

A quiet, pattery rain falls outside. The sky is soft, and the clouds are low and smoky gray. Winston is still snoring down the hall, and I am smearing raspberry jam onto a piece of toast.

Dad shoulders in through the front door, drops a pile of mail onto the corner of the table, and stands there, studying a letter. He holds it out to me, the weight of it sagging the far corner.

The return address says "Ty."

Nothing else. No city, no street—just a long tail on the y that pulls me in and leaves me hanging.

I hate it. Love it. I want to tear it apart and drink it in and ignore it all at the same time.

I sigh. What's next, a dancing telegram from Billie? A

giant gorilla that would dance around on the doorstep and accidentally mash my toes?

I pin the unopened letter to the tabletop with my fingertips and look up at Dad.

"What do you think?" I ask, suddenly feeling that my house may be built of straw.

He turns and reaches for a coffee cup.

"I think he's a boy," he says, slowly filling his cup from the pot before he turns back to me, "and boys fuck up."

He crosses the room with steam swirling between his hands.

"And Billie?"

"Well . . ." He drags out the chair across from me and sits down. "Billie was always going to be Billie."

The clock on the wall over his head ticks quietly. It has a picture of a cup of coffee on it at twelve o'clock. I've heard the phone ringing in the kitchen every night since we got back, well after the house is still and silent, picked up before I can accept the sound as real and untangle myself from my sheets.

"Anytime you want," I've heard him say in the quiet darkness. "Always."

He probably sends her money, listens to her stories, rubbing his tired hands together in the dark, trusting that someday she will find her way home.

"I just thought he was someone else," I say, and I don't

even try to hide the pain from my face. But I can't say the rest, so I think it: someone stronger, braver, truer.

Dad crosses his arms. His eyes grow distant.

"You should always try to see someone for who they are, Teddy Lee," he says, "not who you want them to be."

I watch him sip his coffee. My mom is here with him, leaning over his shoulder, refilling a cup that is pretty much already full.

Would he let her back in? If he were the one sitting here holding a letter, would he want to hear what she had to say? I want to hope so.

"Are all the memories bad?" I ask.

He waits. "That would make it so much easier, wouldn't it?"

I reach for the letter and nod. Yes. Yes, it would.

I am in the garage that night, stumbling and searching for my gear before it gets too late. My hands are slow and stupid in the cold. I grab the old acoustic guitar with the moon and stars on the strap and set it on the floor while I look for the case.

I only turned one light on when I came in, slowly sliding the dimmer that Jay installed to low, leaving big shadows all around me that are shaped like boxes and tires and teenage boys.

I find the case under some sawhorses marked PUBLIC WORKS DEPARTMENT because Winston is such a klepto. I lower my chin down into my scarf, feeling my own breath warm against my lips as I carefully set the guitar into its cracked leather case and click the latches shut.

My shoulders sag when I pull the guitar case off the sawhorse in front of me. It crunches across the pot stems and seeds sprinkled there.

One of Ginger's bright pink Post-It notes catches my eye as I pass by the workbench on my way to the door. I slide my finger down the marked page. I haven't finished today's theory yet.

I push the door open with my toe. The sky outside is dark and gray and swirling, brewing up a storm. A streak of lightning zaps the sky, hurrying me across the grass toward my car at the edge of the street.

Winston is watching me from the kitchen window, peeking through the curtain, the tip of his cigarette burning orange and bright in a long slat of light.

When the clouds break open, he looks skyward, and I start to run.

It's time to break some hearts.

I do not drive by his house; I don't even think about it. Yet I find myself in a neighborhood that looks a lot like Ty's, where normal people live normal lives and porch lights shine out into the night, leading everybody safely back home.

Stopped at a corner of a tree-lined street in front of a big brick house, I lean forward until I can pull Ty's letter out of my back pocket.

I balance it in my hand, feeling its weight. The sight of his handwriting makes my heart beat faster.

Would it be easier if he had just disappeared? If he had been a person who existed once, had been everything to me once, and then just wasn't?

My light is just beginning to flicker again. It dodges and dashes, fighting against all winds, and I am afraid that one look, one touch, even just one word from Ty will snuff me out.

I let the letter drop on to the seat next to me, and I drive away.

The rain is disappearing into a mist that clings to the road and the tires on the trucks in front of me. I open my window on my way out of town and breathe in deeply.

After exiting on the first ramp that leads toward downtown, I take a right. I follow streets named after presidents and states. I make an entire constitution full of turns and one more right to a street lined with shops and galleries and parking meters planted next to small green trees at the curb.

Driving slowly, I pace a guy in a saggy knit cap and a girl in a flowered skirt and Wellington boots. They rush along the sidewalk, holding hands and bouncing off each other like they are in love.

They disappear behind me as I pull up and park in front

of a coffee shop. The sign above my wet windshield says: OPEN MIC TONIGHT! DOORS AT 9! I sit back and watch a small crowd trickle in and out: boys with goatees and girls in socks and sandals.

It's almost eleven when I finally grab for my door handle. I hop across the flooded cracks in the sidewalk and, holding on tight to my guitar case, stop under the awning to wipe the rain from my face.

The place is packed, a jumble of round tables and mismatched chairs on a stained wooden floor. The coffee cups are thick and white, every one resting on a white saucer. The air is heavy, weighted down with talk and the sogginess of the passing rainstorm and the smell of cinnamon.

It is only a small coffee bar in a nearby college town, but still, I have to sign up and wait through two other performers before I get a turn. I follow a girl in a holey sweater who reads some angry poetry.

I climb up onto the stage by myself. It is so tiny I'm not sure you can officially call it a stage. It is more of an apple box with a riser attached to the back. And the crowd is right there, hanging at the tip of my toe when I cross my leg and adjust my guitar.

The sounds of breathing and the scuff of chairs and the whoosh of the espresso machine surround me. The angry poet stands, lips drawn tight, like a fuzzy stalagmite in the back row. Someone close by clears his throat, impatient. I am stalling.

Even if I don't like to admit it to myself, I keep thinking that Billie is going to show up, pull out a chair, and sit down next to me. She'll prop her sparkly guitar between her legs and pretend to play, shining me on, along with everybody else.

Looking up into the single spotlight strung overhead, I gather myself together and start to play. My heart aches for the beat of a drum.

But my guitar fills the room. I sing, softly at first, focusing on the new fingerings that Ginger taught me, leaning hard on one word, drawing out another, moving forward step by step, my voice building as I feel the small space around me expanding, getting bigger and bigger until we are floating, the book-smart girls and the boys who like them, the band geeks with the good haircuts and the knitters and the studiers and the poets and the part-time rappers, we all are swirling together in a twirl of music and magic and steamed milk.

I finish, and the applause drowns out the café noise along with the pounding of my heart. I slide my guitar off my lap and start to rise, aware of a hot rush rising on my cheeks.

"Awww, come on!" somebody yells from a table in the back, sounding exactly like Jay, and my stomach trips over itself. "One more!"

The grad student manning the sign-up sheet nods when

I look over. A girl with a fat, wrinkled journal tugs at her cardigan and sits back down, bumped.

I slide back onto the stool and put my fingers over the frets, thinking.

What song can I pull from the memories and moments that are mashed together in my head? I wasn't expecting an encore. Then it comes to me: an arrangement that Ginger and I have been working on in the garage. It is supercheesy and completely unexpected and totally perfect. It is "Faith."

I start, close and low at first, then louder and louder, until my voice is clear and strong and steady, and I am so excited that I desperately need to swallow, but I don't.

I strum and I sing and I feel the tiny gusts of air from hands clapping to the beat around me. A blonde on my right is singing along. A silver bracelet twinkles on her wrist.

There are times in your life that you know are good. They sparkle and glow. This is one of them. Everything is rich and saturated and absorbing, yet somehow I feel separate, as if I were watching every moment from above, with the color turned up. Every single second is sharp, with slanting light like an autumn day and a crisp, sweet breeze. Life crackles under my feet.

When the applause starts to thunder, I can breathe. I set my guitar at my side and smile out at the crowd.

I uncross my legs and rise out of my chair to cheers and glowing phones and one of those wolf whistles that streaks over the top of the crowd. The poet in the back looks like she might be on the verge of happy; her mouth is starting to curve up at the corners.

I do a strange kind of bow, or maybe you can call it a curtsy, as the applause fades away and I stand in the light.

21

I drive through the rain after my set at the coffee shop, steering my car past neon exits and all-night truck stops. I pass the first place we ever played and Randy's radio station, the place where we started.

I turn down our street with no curbs, just gravel and grass, back toward home. I cross cracked linoleum, worn carpet, and a soft triangle of light on a pink rug. The quilted kittens stand by as I drop my bag and return my guitar to the corner of my room so the moon and stars can watch over me, shining.

I crawl under my covers and snuggle myself in tight, a new song starting in my head. It's the one about falling hard and forgiveness and soft green palm fronds resting on the ground behind me. Then I close my eyes and I sink, into a downy pillow, a warm quilt, a sweet song.

I sleep with the door open.

The coffeepot gurgles on the counter the next morning. Dad is at the table, watching it bubble. Winston is one seat down, drawing mustaches on the underwear models in a catalog with a ballpoint pen, his knee bouncing under the table.

Padding across the cool floor in bare feet, I think about finding a spoon, maybe some juice. A light is on in the garage, beaming out into the foggy backyard.

I stop in front of the fridge.

A strip of pictures—the kind you get from a photo booth at the mall or a tourist trap—is slipped under the edge of the magnet that holds up our growing grocery list.

Billie and Ben.

Billie and Glen.

Billie and all the Blasting Cap boys crammed into the photo booth. One of the boys is only a skinny tattooed shoulder in that shot, another boy just a blur of dark hair and a frozen arm tucked into the lower corner.

The last one is Billie, by herself. She smiles back at me in a bright coral T-shirt, waving at the camera. Where did she manage to find a stamp?

I slip the strip of photos out from under the list. The top edge is bent and wrinkled, probably from being jammed into a back pocket and then into an envelope. I nudge it toward the middle of the fridge with my fingertip, and then set a magnet at the top, so we all can see her.

Dad slides out of his seat. He walks up beside me and rests his warm, rough hand on the top of my shoulder. Reaching past the care package he is building for Billie on the countertop—quarters for her laundry, candy to rot her teeth, and a pair of warm socks I know she'll never wear—to straighten the photos.

He centers the magnet.

"Who's making the eggs?" he asks.

Winston stops, mid-mustache and points at me.

"Of course." Dad laughs, grabbing the big glass bowl from the highest shelf and handing it to me.

We have scrambled eggs with toast and jelly.

22

We are in the garage, just Ginger and me. It's cold and sunny, the start of winter. We both are wearing hoodies, but Ginger has his sleeves pulled up, probably because his arms are so long. Dust floats in the sunshine between us.

My head is bent low over my guitar. Ginger's knees are angled toward mine, facing the open garage door.

"Can I just play a little bit of it on my own?" I say to him, not noticing his stillness, the fact that he has stopped playing. "Just to get the—"

I lift my chin. Birds had been chirping. The street had been buzzing and whirring with the sounds of husbands who have been locked inside the house for too long. I swear it all has stopped.

Ginger's hand hovers over his strings, quiet. I sit up and shiver.

Ty is walking up the driveway, slow and straight. He looks thin. Clean. Scrubbed somehow. As if he has been through some serious shit, something that drained him but left him stronger. Like leeches or a bloodletting of some sort.

The driveway draws out, becoming longer, the space between us immeasurable. I want to run to him in slow motion, a chariot of fire on a wet gravel path.

Ginger puts his guitar down and stands. I am still sitting.

I am a statue. Lungless. Breathless.

Here he is, on a random Tuesday afternoon. It should be an auspicious date with double digits and flags out on the street, or a full moon at the very least.

My heart is a hummingbird trapped in my chest.

Ginger and Ty smile at each other and shake hands.

I don't really know what to do. I've never had anybody come back before.

I set my guitar down at my side.

Ginger ducks under the open garage door and reappears, even taller, with his gold ten-speed between his legs. He waves, rolling across the yard and toward the street.

Ty is wearing a black T-shirt under his tan jacket. When he moves closer to me, I spy a little red cupcake silk-screened on the pocket over his heart, and I push Ginger's empty chair toward him with my foot.

Without hesitating, he takes a seat and reaches for Ginger's guitar. He slides the strap over his neck then stretches his legs out in front of him, first things first.

He starts to strum lightly.

"Ginger told me what you have been up to," he says as I follow along.

Watching his fingers warming up with chords and slides, I let the soft sounds flow and melt into me as I soak in the arc of his shoulders, the timbre of his voice, the substance and shape and smell of him.

Ty slows and then stops completely, waiting for me.

I grab my guitar and glide right into the middle of a song, catching him by surprise. It's a song that was born in my bedroom and brought to life in a motel in the middle of a summer's night, a song of lamplight and soft guitar, a song of longing and absolution, a song of mine.

He looks over at me, his eyes golden, bright, and sure.

"Where you start isn't always the beginning, is it?" he asks.

I smile, leading him back in.

I sing while shooting stars dance and glimmer behind my eyes, lighting me up. We start again.